FEDERAL FAG

STONEWALL INN MYSTERIES
KEITH KAHLA, GENERAL EDITOR

Sunday's Child by Edward Phillips
Sherlock Holmes and the Mysterious Friend of Oscar Wilde
by Russell A. Brown
A Simple Suburban Murder by Mark Richard Zubro
A Body to Dye For by Grant Michaels
Why Isn't Becky Twitchell Dead? by Mark Richard Zubro
Sorry Now? by Mark Richard Zubro
Love You to Death by Grant Michaels
Third Man Out by Richard Stevenson
Principal Cause of Death by Mark Richard Zubro
Political Poison by Mark Richard Zubro
Brotherly Love by Randye Lordon
Dead on Your Feet by Grant Michaels
On the Other Hand, Death by Richard Stevenson
A Queer Kind of Love by George Baxt
An Echo of Death by Mark Richard Zubro
Ice Blues by Richard Stevenson
Mask for a Diva by Grant Michaels
Sister's Keeper by Randye Lordon
Another Dead Teenager by Mark Richard Zubro
Shock to the System by Richard Stevenson
Let's Get Criminal by Lev Raphael
Rust on the Razor by Mark Richard Zubro
Time to Check Out by Grant Michaels
Chain of Fools by Richard Stevenson
Government Gay by Fred Hunter
The Truth Can Get You Killed by Mark Richard Zubro
The Edith Wharton Murders by Lev Raphael
Federal Fag by Fred Hunter
Are You Nuts? by Mark Richard Zubro
Dead as a Doornail by Grant Michaels

FEDERAL FAG

Fred Hunter

ST. MARTIN'S PRESS
NEW YORK

Library of Congress Cataloging-in-Publication Data

Hunter, Fred.
    Federal fag / Fred Hunter.
        p. cm.
    ISBN 0-312-18580-4 (hc)
    ISBN 0-312-20649-6 (pbk)
    I. Title.
    PS3558.U476F44   1998
    813'.54—dc21

                                                98-4993
                                                CIP

First Stonewall Inn Edition: May 1999

10 9 8 7 6 5 4 3 2 1

For Raymond Dragon

FEDERAL FAG

I don't usually rent porno movies. The only reason I fell from grace that particular evening was that Peter had gone to his high school reunion without me. Most people would be relieved at not being required to attend such a function, but with me it was different: Peter didn't want me to go because he didn't want to introduce his old classmates to his husband. He did go so far as to allow me to accompany him to Los Angeles, with the promise that we'd spend the week after vacationing in the sun and sand.

But his refusal to take me to the actual event still rankled and caused what was, for us, a rare argument. I was in an untenable position, since I felt snubbed by not being taken to an event that I didn't really want to attend—but there was a principle at work here. I thought it was ludicrous for Peter to leave me behind given that all of his high-school buddies had known at the time that he was gay. Peter was out of the closet before he'd even realized he

1

was supposed to be in one. He explained that although most everyone had been cool about his sexuality when he was in high school, liberal children have a habit of growing up into adults who are middle-class in the worst way, and he had no intention of subjecting me (or himself) to the "hoots and sniggers" of people who weren't worth my time. Besides, he added, I'd just be bored. Of course, the only possible response for me to make to that was "Then why the hell do *you* want to go?" He'd replied with a shrug, "They were my friends." All this boiled down to the fact that it was simply easier on him to go to the reunion without me.

So there I was on Saturday evening, alone in our room at the Hotel Windemere by the Sea in Santa Monica, with Peter off to see his classmates and my mother two thousand miles away in our town house in Chicago.

I'd selected a video with the auspicious title *Big Tools of the Trade*. I popped it into the VCR that came with the room in our fairly classy digs. The usual disclaimer about all actors in the video being eighteen or older popped on the screen and I smiled at the use of the term "actor." While the opening credits ran, I slipped out of my clothes and dropped onto the bed, nestling in the rose-colored sheets. Satin can be very comforting when you're feeling sorry for yourself.

Suffice it to say that, to put it as delicately as possible, the first "encounter" took care of my needs, and I went to wash up, neglecting to stop the VCR. When I came back into the room, one of the hotel's semi-plush white towels wrapped around my waist, I was about to stop and rewind the tape when I glanced at the TV. Three young men were going through a series of acrobatics in an apparent attempt to prove they could somehow find physical satisfaction while defying gravity. Something about the scene seemed really strange to me, besides what they were doing. There was something vaguely familiar about one of the men. I sat on the edge of the bed and peered closely at the set. The camera switched from a long shot of the three of them to a close-up of the man in the middle as he performed the sexual equivalent of burning the candle at both ends. And then it struck me: it was Patrick Gleason. I'd gone to college with him.

I told myself I was shocked, and that I wasn't turned on—despite the physical evidence to the contrary. I'd always believed that people who fucked for the camera only existed on celluloid, and it was unnerving to have it proven otherwise. It was the same feeling I had when I was in high school and ran into Mr. Fredrickson, my freshman English teacher, in a grocery store. I had pretty vocally expressed surprise at seeing him there, to the point that he gave me a rather withering look and exclaimed, "Teachers eat, too, you know."

In fact, I was so stunned to find Patrick Gleason indecorously sandwiched between two nubile youths, I thought that maybe my eyes were deceiving me—a possibility, since, at those angles, it was kind of hard to be sure. I fast-forwarded to the end of the tape, where they sometimes have a "cast list" with pictures. Slowly, to the beat of some innocuous pseudo-jazz, a list of players went by, each displayed in turn in full-frontal-nude shots with their "names" across the bottom of the screen. Of course, their names were purely fictitious, to protect the guilty: there was "Rock Hardin," "Ted Manly," and a couple of other young surfer types with equally adolescent pseudonyms.

3

Then the man I was looking for flashed onto the screen: "Butch Handy." He had long blond hair, light blue eyes, and a thin layer of chest hair that started at his nipples and ran down to a point at his navel like a fur triangle. He had picked a particularly ironic moniker: he was anything but butch. In fact, he was rather pretty in an angular sort of way. If there had been any doubt in my mind that this was my old college buddy Patrick Gleason, it was dispelled by the sight of the tiny shamrock tattooed on his right pelvic bone. I remembered it.

"So how was it?" I said as Peter sat on the end of the bed and took off his shoes.

"Boring," he replied. "Everybody was pretty much the way I remembered them."

He sounded despondent and distracted, which is probably the way most people respond to their high school reunions. I avoid my own like the plague because they only serve to foster the idea that nobody ever achieves what they set out to do. Failure is the theme of the party. For Peter, the worst part about it was that he couldn't tell them the one really impressive thing that had happened to him of late: that along with me he'd become a part-time spy. Peter and I inadvertently became mixed up in the middle of a government operation involving a kidnapping ring in Russia. After we proved instrumental in breaking it up, Lawrence Nelson, the government agent with whom we'd worked, had sort of drafted us as "occasional agents." Since then our assignments had been few and far between and pretty innocuous, although I did once get to fly to New York to meet a visiting agent from another country (I had no need to know which one) and make sure that he caught his connecting flight to Washington. Nothing a good sky-cap couldn't have done.

Peter kicked his shoes and socks into a corner of the room, then got up and stripped off his pants and shirt. As he carefully slid his silk shirt onto a hanger and transferred it to the closet, I marveled again at how beautiful he is. His loose-fitting khaki boxer shorts complemented his olive skin and showed off his sleek, muscular legs; his stomach is flat but it hasn't been exercised into something threatening, and his chest is tight. He has a dark head of hair that tends to be curly, and deep, green eyes that I can feel caressing me before we make contact.

"What did you do with yourself all evening?" he asked in a tone that implied he was prepared for me to whine again about being left behind. He didn't know how ironic the question was.

"Uh . . . nothing really . . ." I glanced at the television set. "I have something to show you."

"What?"

"Well, while you were out tonight I rented a movie."

"You did?"

I turned on the VCR and the TV. I glanced back over my shoulder and said, "Um, sort of a movie . . . I rented this and got the surprise of my life. Somebody I went to college with is in it."

"You're kidding!"

"He's only in part of it," I replied, already regretting that I hadn't approached this more directly. "You have to see this."

I pressed the play button on the VCR and stood back.

I had rewound the tape to the middle of Patrick Gleason's scene, which now popped onto the screen at a point where the three participants were going at it with calculated abandon.

Peter was silent, his arms folded across his chest. His expression was inscrutable. After a moment, he said, "You rented a porno movie?"

I realized at once that it would be folly to deny it as the erect bodies slapped against each other on the screen.

"Well, you were gone," I said weakly.

"You came all the way to Los Angeles to rent a prono movie?"

"No," I said, "I came here to be with you."

Another silence followed, which I found a little more unsettling than the first because I thought just maybe I'd gone too far. Finally he said, "Which one is your friend?"

"The one in the middle."

In a really inauspicious bit of timing, my former college-mate chose that moment to moan "Oh God, oh God."

Peter pulled a slow take at me, the right side of his lip curling wryly.

"You say you went to college with him? That was over ten years ago."

"Yeah," I said, glancing at the TV, "he's a little old for porno movies."

"So are you," he replied, his voice taking on an uncharacteristic, unattractive edge.

"It's not like you've never rented one."

Peter sighed and put his arms around my neck. He smiled with that glint in his eyes that I found so attractive and said, "You know that since we've been together I've been

6

satisfied to live one rather than rent one." He kissed my nose lightly. "Are you still mad at me for going without you?"

I made a show of thinking about that for a second. "Naw."

"Well, you were right. I should have taken you with me. I would have had somebody interesting to talk to . . . or at least to laugh at everybody with."

"You're not really upset because I rented that, are you?"

He glanced at the screen, shrugged, and said, "You're a big boy. You get to do whatever you want."

"Really?" I said.

Our lips met. As I slid my hands down into his shorts, I heard the TV snap off. I don't know how he reached the remote.

We lay together for a while in the afterglow, Peter gently rolling my hair in his fingers. I let out a contented sigh and said, "That was really weird."

"Thanks," he said, a smile in his voice.

"I mean . . . I mean finding Pat Gleason in a porno movie."

Peter's fingers stopped their gentle twining of my hair. After a moment he said, "Why? Wasn't he the type?"

"Well, I don't exactly know what type of person would end up in that kind of movie, but no, I don't think he was. He slept around in college, but everybody did."

"Really?" he said with feigned shock.

"All I'm saying is, Pat was no worse than anybody else in the bed department."

Peter craned his neck over to look at my face, his expression one of profound perplexity.

"I mean in terms of sheer numbers," I amended hastily.

"Oh," he replied, resting his head back against his pillow. "And were you that active in college?"

I glanced at him to see whether or not he was serious. This was an area we seldom approached. "Nope. I was shy."

We lay there silently for a few moments. Peter went back to giving me a finger wave while I gently stroked his left nipple with my thumb.

"You know," I said, breaking the companionable silence, "I'm worried about him."

"What?"

"Patrick. When I knew him he wanted to be an actor really badly. That's how I met him. He was in a student production of *Fiorello* that I designed the sets for. He was serious about acting."

"The one performance I caught was very convincing."

I shook my head lightly, my hair brushing against his cheek. I knew I should let the subject drop, but I just couldn't. "I can't believe he's making porn. He must've known that once he'd done it, he'd have no chance of a mainstream acting career. Things must've gotten pretty bad for him to throw everything away like that."

"Then again," said Peter in that same opaque tone, "maybe he just likes it."

I pondered this, along with what Patrick had been like when I'd known him. It would be convenient enough for me to believe that Peter was right, but, since the memory of my relationship with Patrick still hurt, I had to distrust my own feelings. After a long silence, I said tentatively, "Peter . . . the credits on that tape say it was made in Los Angeles. I think maybe . . . I'll look Patrick up while we're here."

"What? Why?"

"Because I'm worried about him. Maybe I can help him."

"Yeah, right."

"I mean it, Peter," I said defensively. "I'm worried about him. You know what that life is like."

"No, I don't. And you don't either . . . I hope."

Ignoring the last, I said, "I mean, you've heard what that life is like—it's dangerous: drugs, disease, and, if you can believe the scuttlebutt, the Mob is involved in the porn industry."

" 'The Mob'?" said Peter, apostrophizing the words in a way designed to make me blush. I was angry that he succeeded.

"The Mob, organized crime, whatever you want to call it."

"And you're going to try to *save* this old friend of yours?"

"You don't have to be so damn melodramatic. Not *save* him, but help if I can. You know as well as I do that if our positions were reversed—I mean yours and mine—that you'd try to do something for him."

I had him there, and he knew it. Truth to tell, Peter is more like me than either of us would care to admit. In fact, he would normally be the first one to let his compassion get the best of his reason. He stared at me for a couple of moments, then said, "You're right, I would." He rolled over on his side, pulling the satin sheet up over his naked shoulder. "That doesn't mean I have to like it."

TWO

Our usual morning ritual of dressing together was performed with the formality of business travelers forced to share a room. We had a quiet breakfast on the balcony overlooking the ocean, then Peter announced he was going for a walk along the beach, presumably because he didn't want to sit in the room and listen while I called Patrick.

Directory assistance didn't have a listing for him either under his own name or his "stage" name. I decided to give Mother a call and enlist her aid.

"What is it, darling?" Her accent was heightened by the feeling that something must be amiss. My mother is British and moved to America when she married my father, whom she later divorced, not terribly long before he was killed in an auto accident. She sustains herself on the proceeds of the insurance policy and inheritance he left her due to the fact that he'd neglected to change beneficiaries after the divorce. "Is anything wrong?"

"Um, no, it's just that I saw this movie last night."

I stopped out of embarrassment. I didn't exactly know how to go about explaining to my mother that I'd been watching a porno movie.

"You most likely could've waited till you came home to tell me that, luvey," she said after a pause.

"Well, see . . . an old friend of mine was in it."

"Really?"

"It wasn't the kind of movie you'd be happy to find a friend in."

For a moment I thought the line had gone dead; then the sound of the light dawning poured through the receiver. "Oooooooooooh."

"It was Patrick. Patrick Gleason. Do you remember him?"

"Little Pattie Gleason?" said Mother gleefully, her choice of words accentuating her very British accent, "Of course I remember him! I used to lunch with his mother." There was another slight pause, and I could just imagine her face clouding over and she added, "You mean he's making dirty pictures? I thought more of him than that. He was so clean."

"Could you do me a favor?" I asked tentatively, "Could you see if directory assistance in Chicago has him listed? I think he's living out here, but he's not listed, so I'm thinking he may have moved back there. If he's not in the book, maybe you could call his mother and find out if she has his phone number."

There was a pause, this one more pregnant than the last; then she said, "What's up with you, Alex?"

I sighed. "You know how close Pat and I were in college."

"I remember the two of you stopped speaking to each other for reasons you kept to yourself."

"Well," I said, choosing my words carefully, "even if we had a falling-out, I feel like I should help him."

"How?"

"I don't know how. But I can at least talk to him. Find out what's going on, and see if there's anything I can do."

There was a long silence. "Are you sure that's all there is to it?"

"Of course. What do you mean?"

She sighed heavily. "I'm sure I don't know what I mean. I'll see what I can do."

She called back later that day to tell me she'd struck out on both counts: Patrick wasn't listed in Chicago, and his mother had been very cagey about his whereabouts. Mother was convinced that Patrick's family either didn't know where he was, or didn't want to know.

"Or maybe he's ashamed of what he's doing and he's fallen out of contact with them," she surmised. Then she added, with a playful lilt in her voice, "Darling, please promise me that if you ever turn to making dirty pictures you'll fall out of contact with me!"

"I promise," I said with a laugh.

"And I'll see if I can't find some way to locate Patrick while you're still out there."

I racked my brain trying to think of who might know how to reach Patrick. Unfortunately, the only person who repeatedly came to mind was Jimmy Bender. Jimmy is the type of person who makes my teeth ache: an innuendo queen. No comment is so innocent that it can't be given an obscene spin. In normal conversation, he's so busy delivering double entendres that he barely has time to breathe. That may be mildly amusing in an evening Noël Coward, but a steady diet of it is just tiresome. In a queen, it can be exhausting. Unfortunately, I had to try him because he'd been a pretty good friend of Patrick's in college, and I was running out of options.

"Why, girlfriend," said Jimmy in his most mincing tone when he realized who was on the phone, "where've you been? I haven't heard from you since God was a chile! You been keeping it greased up?"

I'd forgotten just how offensive I found this kind of banter, not because I'm overly sensitive but because it's so damn pointless and seems to soil everything. When you're in your teens that kind of thing may seem daring, but in your thirties it seems like arrested development. I had half a mind to just say "Forget it" and hang up, but if I were to track down Patrick, I couldn't afford the luxury.

"I'm fine, Jimmy," I said flatly in an attempt to keep his effluvia to a bare minimum, "and I'm calling from Los Angeles."

"La-La Land?" he said with incredulous femininity. "Whatcha doin' out there?"

"Snark hunting," I said, losing my ability to hide my irritation.

"To what do I owe the honor of this long-distance love call? You don't even call when you're at home."

"I was thinking of looking up Patrick while I was out here. Patrick Gleason. I was wondering if you might know how I could get in touch with him."

There was a lurid pause over the line, and I could just

hear the naughty little wheels and gears turning in Jimmy's head.

"Well, girl, I thought that was all over and done with," he said with a smirk in his voice.

"It is," I replied. "I just want to get in touch with him."

"Don't we *all*, sweetie. I understand it's pretty easy."

The way he said this startled me. It occurred to me that just possibly Jimmy knew about Patrick's newfound career. Perhaps he'd happened upon one of Pat's "performances" much in the way I had. Then again, Patrick might have just told him about it.

"Why do you say that?" I asked, hoping he would admit if he had seen the video.

"Oh . . ." he said, milking it for whatever it was worth, "you know, girl, everybody in school wanted a piece of him." Then he added, with a malicious edge, "And from what I heard, just about everybody got it!"

"So you don't know where he is," I said, anxious to get to the point and get off the phone.

"Last I heard, he went to L.A. to seek his fame and fortune. And dahling, with an ass like his he's sure to find it. All he has to do is wag his lily-white tail to get all the parts he wants, if you know what I mean."

"Do you have his address and phone number?"

A little laugh swarmed its way to me through the phone, then a deep breath. Clearly enjoying himself, Jimmy replied, "You know, honey, you really, really should get a grip on yourself and try to loosen your load. You're so tense! Making the scene with some Vaseline might help."

My face went hot with the effort to maintain some semblance of patience. "Look, Jimmy, I just thought you were a friend of his—"

15

"A *friend*," he said in that same insinuating tone, "Oh, no no no, dahling. I never once put a lick to that stick. I wasn't anywhere *near* as close to him as you were."

It was at that moment that the reason for his slightly malicious tone became clear to me, though I must've been a complete idiot for having it take so long: he was jealous. He'd apparently wanted Patrick in a way that wasn't fulfilled. It would've been useless to try to convince Jimmy he was better off.

I said with exaggerated patience, "Jimmy, do you have his address and phone number, or don't you?"

He emitted a hot sigh and said, "Oh, well, I can give you the last ones I have. Keep strokin' it a minute."

I was kept waiting more than a minute, which I suspected was intentional, but I was in no position to complain. He came back to the phone at last and rattled off a phone number and an address in Santa Monica in a tone that clearly implied that he thought that I was robbing him of a john. I quickly scribbled the information on a notepad. I didn't want to have to ask him to repeat it.

"I wonder why it wasn't listed," I said, forgetting my resolve to end the conversation as quickly as possible.

"I think it was under somebody else's name. I think he *had* someone, if you know what I mean."

"Well, thanks," I said curtly.

"Give him a good one for me" was the reply.

I hung up.

To my husband's increasing consternation, I tried Patrick's number several times over the next couple of days, each time getting an answering machine. I didn't leave a message because I didn't want to announce myself that way. It

16

was possible that if he knew I was trying to contact him, he might never pick up the damn phone. In between attempts to reach Patrick I went sightseeing with Peter, who try as he might couldn't hide the fact that he wasn't too thrilled with my new "hobby." I couldn't exactly blame him, but at the same time I found it more and more hard to understand. I've never given Peter any reason for jealousy. With my unhealthy sense of self-doubt, I didn't even think it was possible for me to do that. This was a side of Peter I'd never seen, and if I hadn't been so distressed by it, I would've been flattered.

It wasn't until early on the morning of the third day that Patrick finally answered the phone himself with a groggy "Yeah?"

"Patrick? Patrick, it's me, Alex."

"Alex?"

"Alex Reynolds."

There was a short pause, and then his voice took on a bit more life. There was no doubt in my mind that the realization of who was calling had startled him from his half-waking state a little more quickly than normal.

"Where are you? What are you doing?"

"As it happens," I said with practiced nonchalance, "I'm in the neighborhood. I'm visiting Los Angeles."

"How did you get my number?"

"From Jimmy Bender."

There was a brief pause during which I was unsure whether Patrick was angry with Jimmy for giving me his number, or angry with himself for having picked up the phone.

"It was the last number for you he had," I said, breaking the silence and hoping to smooth over any rough spots, "so he told me to try it. I hope that isn't a problem. I mean, Jimmy knew you and I had been friends, so he didn't see anything wrong with giving your number out to me."

"No, no. It's fine. Of course. I just wondered, you know. Um. It's nice to hear from you."

"Yeah," I said, continuing to try sounding more relaxed than I felt, "I was hoping to get together with you to catch up."

There was another pause, a sure sign that I'd really caught him off guard. He said slowly, "Oh, I don't know, I'm awfully busy, you know."

"I know you are, but I've come all this way."

"To see me?"

"No, no," I said anxiously, "just to vacation, among other things. I thought it would be nice to see you since I was here."

"Well, like I said—"

I cut him off. "Come on, Pat, it wouldn't be any trouble for me to stop by for a little while. If I understand my directions out here correctly, I'm not staying too far from where you live. Won't you at least let me stop by?"

There was that damn pause again. When he replied, there was a hesitation in his voice that he quickly tried to overcome.

"Oh . . . that would be nice, but I have a better idea. We should meet for lunch instead. That would be fun. It'd be like old times, right?"

Old times? Maybe I'd oversold myself here. I didn't want things to be like old times.

"Lunch would be fine with me. When and where?"

"Today," he said, so hurriedly I had no choice but to believe that he was anxious to have it over with, "at noon at Bixby's. It's a sunny little place on Wilshire."

"Noon, then," I said, and we both hung up.

"That was an odd conversation," said Peter. "It sounded almost as if your old friend wasn't too happy to hear from you."

"If it sounded like that just from hearing my side of the conversation, you should have heard his."

"Maybe he has a boyfriend," said Peter with the faintest hint of irony in his voice. It was a clear sign to me of just how frustrated he was with this situation. Usually, even if he's feeling bitter or ironic, he does his best to keep from sounding snide.

"It's possible. But what of it? He can't possibly think I want him back."

"You didn't say why you really wanted to see him," Peter replied, "so he's free to think anything he pleases."

"No," I said, looking him squarely in the eyes, "he really can't think I want him back."

Peter declined to accompany me to this lunch, explaining that whatever I felt needed to be said to Patrick would better be said alone (he added, with an attempt at a smile, that he would feel like one paramour too many). He planned to amuse himself by basking in the sun with a good book. For a split second, I wondered if he was letting me know that, unlike *some* people, when left to himself, he was capable of engaging in healthy pursuits. But I wrote that off as my imagination.

I arrived at Bixby's shortly before noon. I'd dressed discreetly in a pair of jeans and a light blue gauze shirt. I

19

didn't want to look as if I were dressing up for Patrick, but at the same time didn't want to look out of place in California. I ended up looking like what I was: a Chicagoan in costume. I'd neglected to ask whether we should meet inside or out, but since it was pretty hot already I opted to go ahead and get a table.

Patrick had been right to describe this as a sunny restaurant. The walls were all painted bright white, and the ceiling consisted mainly of an enormous skylight. Small white café tables of the type that make you feel as if you're constantly in danger of knocking something over the edge were scattered at indiscreet intervals, and huge potted plants were everywhere. It gave the impression of an outdoor café while being protected from the elements. It was more like a movie set than a restaurant. I hated it.

A cursory glance around the room showed that the tables were beginning to fill up, so I asked the host for a table for two, explaining that I would be joined momentarily. He showed me to one that was partially shielded by an enormous rubber tree and pressed up against a wall in which was carved a fireplace that, to my surprise, bore evidence of recent use. The host left me with two menus and the promise that "Manny" would be by to see to our drinks.

Manny showed up promptly, clad in white from head to toe like all the other wait staff. He had long hair, fashionably bleached blond with dark roots and tied in a ponytail with a puffy cord. His smile looked like it was practiced at night in front of a mirror. He asked me with overt friendliness if I'd like something from the bar. I really thought it best not to have any alcohol, so I asked for a Coke, and told him that somebody would be joining me shortly.

I sat quietly for a while, watching the other restaurant patrons and developing something of an inferiority complex. Bixby's seemed to be the haunt of the very beautiful, or at least the very well put together. I was reminded of an actress I once saw interviewed who said that if she was having a bad hair day she wouldn't leave home. Surveying the denizens of this place, I could see why. I've been told by disinterested parties that I'm fairly presentable, but these people were so well appointed that I felt like I'd just grown a hunch. They all seemed to be going out of their ways not to notice anybody else, while shooting surreptitious glances around the room to check the competition.

I was partially hidden by the giant plant, but I had a clear view of the door. After I'd been there about ten minutes, Patrick came in, pausing for a second as if he was expecting applause. I used the few moments before he discovered me to take a good look at him. The years had been extremely kind. He'd always been good looking, but now he was unnaturally beautiful, and unnaturally thin, and unnaturally blond. The blond part might have been due to the fact that he was sporting a very dark tan. I've always thought that dark tans made fair-skinned people look erotic.

He was decked out in California pastels: very light green shorts, a multicolored shirt of some sort of lightweight material so sheer you could have counted the hairs on his chest. If he got caught in the rain he'd look like an ad for a men's fragrance.

At last he spotted me and headed for the table. He smiled as I rose and extended my hand. To my surprise, he ignored it, slipped his arms around me, and gave me a quick peck on the cheek. He smelled faintly of some sort of flower, the name of which escaped me at the moment.

"It's so good to see you," he said professionally as we took our seats.

"Same here," I said, feeling quite at a loss for words.

Manny reappeared and asked Patrick what he'd like. When Patrick looked up at him and asked for a white wine, Manny did a double-take, then in a flurry of recognition said, "Sure. Right away," and scurried off.

Even if the waiter wasn't familiar with Patrick's "work," I wouldn't have been surprised to see my old college friend eliciting that kind of reaction. On closer look I saw his skin was smooth and clear and completely unlined and un-blemished. In college, he'd definitely been handsome, but he'd still had the gangliness and lack of confidence that come with being in one's late teens or early twenties. Now sexuality seemed to drip from him, as if it were an animal essence over which he had no control. But that didn't mean he was unaware of the effect.

When Manny returned with the wine, I noticed a slight tremor in his hand. He said he'd be back to take our food order, but Patrick stopped him by gently laying his left hand on the waiter's arm. Manny reacted to the touch as if it was a pleasant electrical shock. I was reminded of the scene in *Dracula* where, with a mere look, the Count is able to bend a weak-willed usherette to his will. "Oh, if you'd only use your power for good" flitted through my mind.

"I know what I want," said Patrick. "The crabmeat salad." He turned to me. "Does that sound all right?"

"Sure," I replied.

Manny smiled and walked away, scribbling the order down on his pad. He was probably disappointed that Patrick had robbed him of an additional trip to our table.

"So," said Patrick, pulling a pack of cigarettes from his shirt pocket and lighting up, "how do you like L.A.?"

"It's fine," I said. It hadn't escaped me that the tone he'd used was meant to imply that I was some sort of yokel. "I've been here before."

His eyebrows slid upward. "You have? Really? Hmm."

"Oh yes," I replied, "I've been lots of places. I usually bring Uncle Jed and Ellie Mae with me."

There was a hint of condescension in his smile as he took a drag from the cigarette and ostentatiously blew the smoke up into the air.

"Well, you're looking pretty good."

"And you look absolutely marvelous," I replied sincerely.

"I try to keep fit." He tapped an ash into a glass disc on the table. There was a momentary silence, during which he continued to gaze directly at my face in an attitude I could only describe as some sort of challenge. "So, what did you say brought you out here?"

"Oh, my husband went to high school here, and I came with him to his reunion."

There was a pause. "Your *husband*?" said Patrick in a "what a quaint term" tone.

"Peter. He and I have been together for . . . about five years now."

"Really?" he said with another cock of his eyebrows.

"Very happily. He's a wonderful person."

"Was this someone from college?"

I had the curious sensation that I was soiling the memory by relating it to Patrick, but I went ahead anyway. "No. I met Peter at a birthday party we'd both been invited to by different people. It was pretty funny. Up until then I

23

hadn't been looking for anyone, but with Peter and me it was sort of 'love at first sight,' 'eyes meeting across a crowded room' type of stuff."

"The stuff of fairy tales," he said with an unreadable smile.

"What can I say? It happened. You should meet Peter. You'd like him."

Patrick took another drag from his cigarette and performed the same ritual of tilting his head up and blowing the smoke into the air. "You know me," he said. "I've never met a faggot I didn't love."

I was sure he was trying to somehow get a rise out of me, just as I was sure it would've been more accurate for him to say "I've never met a faggot I didn't fuck." He continued to look at me as if checking to see if he was having the desired effect. I couldn't tell whether or not he was disappointed.

Manny returned with our salads, perfunctorily set mine in front of me and then made a show of arranging Patrick's in front of him. He asked Patrick if there was anything else he could do for him, and Patrick smiled at him winningly and said, "No, this is lovely."

Manny returned the smile, then reluctantly swept away from the table.

Patrick rested his burning cigarette on the edge of the table and took a few tentative bites of salad. Then he said, "So, what are you doing for a living now? What did you go into?"

"Commercial art." I was glad we were broaching the subject of livelihood, because I thought it'd give me a natural opening for discussing how he was making his.

"Commercial art," he said, cocking his head at me with

displeased surprise. "*Commercial* art? I never would have thought it."

"Why?"

"I thought you wanted to be a painter."

"I have to make a living."

He snorted disdainfully and said, "In college you were such an 'artiste.' I'm surprised you'd lower yourself."

That's something coming from someone I'd consider a prostitute, I thought, and then had a brief moment of panic that I might have inadvertently said it out loud. Since Patrick was still chewing, I realized I'd kept my thoughts to myself.

"We were a lot of things in college," I said when I'd composed my inner self, "but we grow out of them."

"Or sell out," he said with his mouth full, almost as an aside that he'd meant me to hear. "Do you work for some company?"

"No, I have a business of my own. I freelance."

"Hmm," he said, managing to infuse the one syllable with disdain.

We ate in silence for a moment. This was not going the way I'd expected it to. Somehow I'd managed to forget how quickly this man could put me on the defensive. I reminded myself of my purpose in coming here, and asked him as nonchalantly as I could, "So, how is your career going?"

"My career?" he said cagily as he licked a bit of crab-meat from his lower lip.

"I thought you came out here to pursue your acting career."

"This is the only place to do it."

"So how's it going?"

He continued to eat as he answered this, his movements and facial expressions taking on the quality of stage business.

"Well, it's rough going even for me, but I have a lot of projects in development. And I get a fair amount of work—actually, I probably get more work than most. I've been in a couple of films. . . ."

"Really?" I said. "Anything I would have seen?"

He laughed in a deprecating manner that told me that his work was a bit too high-flown to attract the likes of me. "Not likely. One of my films has been released in Europe, and from what I hear it's very popular, but it hasn't been released in the U.S. The other is still in postproduction, so nobody's seen it yet. It should be out early next year."

"What's the title?"

His face screwed up attractively as if he were making an effort to recall something unimportant, "Hmmm . . . there was a working title, which I don't remember, but I'm sure they're not going to use that. I don't think they've chosen the real title yet. I'll be sure and let you know when it's released."

I had no way of knowing whether or not any of this was the truth. I stirred my salad around with my fork. I'd only taken a couple of bites, but my appetite was gone. I don't know what exactly I thought would happen at this meeting. I hadn't expected him to lie, even though, given our past history, that's exactly what I should have expected. I suddenly lost all sense of what I'd hoped to accomplish by seeing him, and I wasn't sure how to proceed without sounding as if I was purposely catching him out.

I set my fork down and folded my hands on the table, leaned in toward him and said as soberly as I knew how, "Patrick, I've seen *Big Tools of the Trade*."

To my surprise, he wasn't taken aback at all. He looked up at me, picked up his still-smoldering cigarette, puffed on it, and said, "So, you've seen my work!"

"Um-hm," I answered vacantly.

"What'd you think?"

Good Christ, it was just like we were back in college and he was asking me what I'd thought of his performance in *Fiorello!*

"Huh?"

"What did you think? How was I?"

I paused for a moment, then said, "Pretty much the way I remembered you."

He laughed merrily and took another puff from his cigarette, blowing the smoke in the air as he slid one elegant leg over the other.

"Good old Alex," he said, smiling broadly, "I never could put anything over on you! You could always see through me."

"Not always."

"So . . . Alex . . . is that why you wanted to see me? Seeing me in the video make you nostalgic?"

I continued to stare at him stupidly. "No. Peter is quite enough for me, thank you."

"Then what? Were you shocked?"

"No."

There was a flicker of disappointment in his face. Then the hint of a smile.

"Did it turn you on?"

"No," I replied, trying desperately to control my flushing cheeks.

"Then what is it? Why did you want to see me?"

I sighed and pulled the cloth napkin from my lap,

balling it up and tossing it into my salad. "Because we were close once. Because I wanted to know what happened."

His face was a mask of perplexity. "What happened? What do you mean?"

"How did you end up doing porn?"

His smile broadened. He leaned in toward me, resting his chin on the hand that held the cigarette so that it looked like smoke was trailing from his ear. "That's so like you. I didn't *end up* doing it, I sought it out. I *love* it! I love fucking men! *You* should know that."

I eyed him a moment, then answered quietly, "Yes, I know."

His eyes narrowed slightly and I could see he was pleased with my reaction. "I can't get enough of it. I mean Alex, baby, I'll be lyin' there in front of the cameras, licking some guy's dick, and all I can think is, Jesus, and I get paid for this, too!" He sat back and tapped his cigarette out in the glass tray, then automatically lit another. "After all, how many people can say that they love what they do for a living?"

Of course, I'd realized by now that this meeting had been a fool's errand. I'd only been able to think of him as having been brought down to the depths because he was doing porn. In whatever emotional upheaval I'd experienced over finding him that way, I'd been blind to the truth of what Peter had said in the first place, when he dismissed the whole issue with a terse "Maybe he just likes it." God, I'd been such an idiot! And it hurt even more because it wasn't the first time I'd been an idiot where Patrick was concerned. Whatever I'd planned to say to him was worthless, because if he truly liked what he was doing, there was certainly nothing I could do to convince him otherwise.

And why should I? I had the embarrassing realization as I sat there listening to him that it was none of my damned business anyway.

"I thought you wanted to be an actor," I said weakly.

"No, baby, I just want to be happy. I wasn't *that* good an actor, anyway."

I looked at him for a moment, sitting there smiling smugly at someone who'd had the audacity to care about him, and said as pointedly as I knew how, "You were a very good actor when I knew you."

Patrick let out a laugh, tapped another ash into the tray, and said, "Let's just say my audience was a little more willing to suspend disbelief than most."

I could feel my face burning again.

"What about money?" I asked, as if having failed to reach him from a moral standpoint I might get him from the practical.

"What do you care?" he replied calmly.

I lowered my head for a moment, noticing how unappealing the addition of my napkin had made my salad. I said quietly, "I just wanted to make sure you were all right."

He pointed to his shirt, shorts, and shoes in turn. "Eighty dollars, sixty dollars, a hundred and twenty dollars."

I got the message. It was no use. This was like trying to convince a pusher that he'd be better off selling insurance. "I guess that's all that matters."

"Hey, I'm popular. I work all the time. Fuck, I've even got a shoot this afternoon."

"I'm sure you're the top in your field."

He remained outwardly calm, even genial; his gestures continued to be fluid and theatrical, but I knew him. The degeneration of his language was a sign that I'd managed to stick a needle in somewhere. "I'm a star. And what the fuck are you? Just a bumfuck little freelance artist."

"That's not all I do," I said, really working at retaining what remained of my dignity.

"Yeah, right. So instead of doing what you want to do, instead of being a *real* artist, you're scratching out a paycheck drawing for dollars."

"That's not all I do," I said so loudly that a finely tuned, thoroughly tanned and lacquered couple at the next table suffered themselves to glance in our direction.

"So what else do you do?" he said, the smug smile returning to his lips.

"I work for the CIA," I blurted out. Horrified, I realized almost at once what I'd said and wished I could call it back, not only because it sounded so positively ludicrous, but because I was never supposed to say anything about it to anyone.

I got exactly the reaction I could expect from Patrick: he was startled for a moment; then he burst out laughing. The mirth seemed to break his part of the tension that had arisen between us. All it managed to do was heighten my confusion.

"Jesus, Alex! You always could make me laugh!"

"Yeah," I said in a weak attempt to recover myself, "I knew that one would get you."

He laughed so hard that his eyes brimmed with tears, which he swept away absently with the hand that held his perpetual cigarette. "So I take it," said Patrick when he'd calmed down and regained a bit of the brashness he'd displayed earlier, "that the real reason you wanted to see me was so's you could try to—what—try to straighten me out?"

It was infuriating to find that after all these years, Patrick could get my goat so completely, and manage to twist my best intentions into something ridiculous. I said, as solemnly as I could, "I just wanted to make sure you were all right."

He leaned in toward me again and said conspiratorially, "Let me set your mind at ease, baby: I'm fine. I'm great. I'm better than ever. And if you had about an hour, we could go back to your hotel room and I'd prove it to you." He made a show of remembering something, slapping his forehead. "Oh, I forgot! The little woman is waiting for you at home."

I stared at him. My face was no longer red. In fact, I don't think I was particularly feeling anything. I pulled a twenty from my wallet and dropped it on the table.

"It was nice seeing you again," I said as I walked away.

Fade to black.

THREE

I returned to our room in a mood that was a mixture of anger and stupor. Peter was sitting on the balcony in a bathing suit, reading the latest Ellen Hart. I stepped up to the railing without a word and gazed out at the ocean, my back to him. He waited a few minutes before he said, "How did it go?"

"I used to love him," I said. I rested my elbows on the railing and propped my chin up on my folded hands. I added, "I mean, I thought I did. It was a long time ago."

Peter was surprised by this admission because neither of us is given to talking much about the past. Through a silent mutual consent we have resolutely steered clear of discussing our past relationships. We're not burying our heads in the sand: we're both well aware that each of us had known other men in the biblical sense before we met. We just think it's best not to discuss old boyfriends in anything other than anecdotal terms, an arrangement that I find perfectly healthy. Peter said nothing, giving me space and time to proceed at my own pace.

"I came out for him, you know," I said.

"I don't understand."

I glanced at him over my shoulder. "I came out for him, in college. I wasn't exactly in the closet, I was just . . . not active. And when I met Patrick, I came out with a vengeance, because I thought I loved him." I sighed and felt as if a hundred years of turmoil were shaking out of me with the action. "He was the first guy I ever slept with. I went with him for, I think, about six months. I was head over heels. And I was sure he loved me, too."

"What happened?"

I shrugged. "Same old story. Like the proverbial wife, I was the last to know he was sleeping with anybody and everybody. And when I found out, I realized that he didn't love me, he just loved sex. That part of him hasn't changed." I let out a rueful little laugh. "You see, I'm so damn middle-class. I was looking for a husband. Like you."

Peter rose and put his hands on my shoulders. "You were mature, sweetheart."

"The amazing thing is, he'd gotten by Mother, too. She met him and liked him. I never told her what happened. All she knew was that I'd stopped seeing him, not the reason why, and she never asked."

"She wouldn't. She has too much sense," he said quietly.

I smiled, but it faded quickly at the memory. "I've never told anybody, because . . . I was just too humiliated."

Peter turned me around and put his arms around my neck, drawing my head down onto his shoulder.

"The worst part is," I continued as I slid my arms around him, "that I never said anything to him, either. I

34

just never had anything to do with him anymore. I never told him what a shit he was."

Peter was silent a moment, tightening his embrace. Then he said, "Maybe that's why you needed to talk to him so badly. Maybe you needed to tell him that."

If that was the case, I still did.

Even though the emotional nature of the day had left me exhausted, I spent most of the night tossing and turning in bed. Peter lay there quietly, but I was certain that he was awake a good deal of the time. By morning I had made a decision: Peter was right. It was time for me to confront Patrick, not about his current affairs, but about those of our past.

Unlike the previous day, Peter offered to come with me (and wait in the car), but I told him that if he'd thought his presence would have been inappropriate at yesterday's lunch, it would be even more so at today's confrontation. And his presence would have made it harder to do without falling apart.

Though it was only about nine in the morning, the sun already seemed high and hot to me as I climbed into our rental car and headed out for Patrick's apartment. The address Jimmy Bender had given me was on Palm Way, a street that proved easy enough to locate and that fully lived up to its name: it was lined on both sides with towering trees with drooping palms. There were brown fronds scattered here and there about the street like large dead animals. The sun was not yet at an angle where it would throw direct light onto the street, and that coupled with the ominously overhanging trees cast a sense of gloom over the area.

I drove slowly up the street, scanning the buildings for the number where Patrick lived. There was a lot of adobe and stucco in evidence, all painted in pastels. All the buildings seemed to have been erected decades ago and had not been touched since. The whole place had a ramshackle, enforested feel. Maybe it was just my mood.

I finally found Patrick's building in the middle of the third block. I parked the car, got out, and went directly to the front door, afraid that any hesitation would weaken my resolve. The general quiet was enough to set my nerves on edge. Though Palm Way was pretty close to a major thoroughfare, it was extremely quiet, the stillness only occasionally interrupted by the loud crack of palm fronds hitting the street. The building was a two-story square painted Pepto-Bismol pink. To the right of the glass doors was a large crack that ran up the side of the wall like a nasty black vine. The doors gave a full view of the enclosed courtyard, which was open to the sky and the elements. A sidewalk snaked around the perimeter of the square and the first-floor apartments opened directly onto it. Instead of the sunniness you might have expected, it was overshadowed by the walkway that circled the second floor. The lock on the glass door was broken, the amount of rust bearing evidence to the fact that it had been in that condition for quite some time.

The door creaked noisily as I swung it open and slammed with the finality of a cell door behind me after I'd stepped through. I started around the walk looking for apartment number 5. Despite the openness of this courtyard, my footsteps echoed loudly. I was surprised by the general dinginess of the place, convinced as I was that

Patrick was making money hand over fist, so to speak. Cracks ran like varicose veins up most of the walls, probably the result of earthquakes, but I was still at a loss for why nothing was done about them. The grass was brown and the halfhearted attempt at a garden had been foiled by an early death: the air was foul with the smell of fetid earth. There was a rustling in a bush that spread under one apartment window, and I was sure I didn't want to know what had caused it.

Each door was covered with cracking paint in a hue just off from the paint on the walls, and each bore a very old, tarnished mock-brass number. I found number 5 in a corner, beneath the stairway to the second floor.

I knocked, but there was no answer. I waited, knocked again, and when there was still no answer I called out, "Patrick, it's me. I want to talk to you." My voice seemed to bounce around the courtyard.

I was rather puzzled because I didn't think he would leave his apartment so early, and that is probably why I tried the door before leaving. To my surprise, it wasn't locked, but swung open readily, banging against the inner wall.

"Patrick, it's Alex! Are you here?"

I was greeted with the kind of silence that rings in your ears. I stepped into the apartment, which was blindingly dark given the general gloominess outside and the cheap, heavy curtains drawn across the one window. I immediately noticed how musty and dank the place smelled, as if decades of moisture had soaked deep into the core of the place and would never be fully extracted. It was a sickly smell that made me feel the way I do back home when using one of the underpasses along Lake Shore Drive to cross over to the lake: like it's unhealthy even to breathe there.

I called to Patrick again and received no answer. I continued carefully into the apartment, my eyes slowly adjusting to the lack of light. The surroundings were, to be really generous, not palatial. To be less generous, the place was squalid. It consisted of one room and a sort of closet that served as the kitchen. There was a filthy shag rug of indeterminate color, which covered only half the room. The furnishings were early college dorm: there was an extremely old white Naugahyde couch with several slashlike tears across its back, a card table with one chair, and a tiny, ancient television set. This apartment was at odds with the successful old friend with whom I'd lunched the day before.

Directly across the room from the front door was the bathroom, the door of which was slightly ajar. I cringed at the thought of the condition the bathroom might be in, but couldn't help myself: I had to look. I pushed the door and it swung open like a curtain going up on a play. There was Patrick. He was naked and lay sprawled in the empty bathtub. There was a bullet hole in his forehead and another in his chest.

In the brief moment before I became paralyzed, I think I half believed that a trick was being played on me, like something out of *Diabolique*. But there was enough physical evidence to convince me otherwise. I froze, unable to move or take my eyes away from the corpse.

It's because of the shock that I didn't become aware of the sound until it was almost upon me, though I realized then that I had heard it somewhere in the back of my mind: there were footsteps echoing through the courtyard. I hadn't shut the door when I came in, and the contents of the bathroom were plainly visible from the front door. I was still frozen when the footsteps reached the door and stopped, but I was jarred from that state when a female voice said in an anxious whisper, "Is he dead?"

I turned and looked at the woman blankly. She was silhouetted in the doorway like an apparition. She was wearing a huge floppy sun hat that had a sheer material over the top and tied around her chin. She also wore some sort of flowing peasant dress type thing that made her seem swathed in cloth rather than dressed in any particular way and served to hide her shape. I thought I must have just happened into a nightmare. The woman remained motionless, like a phantom that had appeared to herald the death, but at the same time she seemed to pulsate with anxiety that somehow seemed to have more to do with discovering me than with the dead body. Though I could see nothing of her face, there was something inexplicably familiar about her. I was so startled I couldn't seem to speak or move.

After a very tense silence, the woman said, "We've got to get out of here!"

And that's when I recognized her.

It was my mother.

FOUR

What in the hell are you doing here?" I demanded incredulously.

She came in and looked into the bathroom. "He *is* dead, isn't he? Oh my goodness!"

"And why are you done up like Mrs. Madrigal?"

"Explanations will have to wait until later. We've got to get out of here."

With this she took hold of my arm and started to steer me out of the apartment, but I shook myself free.

"Are you out of your mind? That's all we need, to be seen fleeing from the scene of a murder!"

Mother clucked her tongue, folded her arms and rested her hand on her chin. She certainly looked as if her mind were racing. "Oh, Lor', I suppose that's true."

As entirely befuddled as I was by Mother suddenly turning up in this almost supernatural fashion, I have to admit I was so relieved I almost wet myself. There is something remarkably comforting about having your mother on hand when you discover a dead porno star.

"I suppose we have to call the police," she said resignedly, "but you know this isn't going to be easy."

"I wish you had a boyfriend on the force here," I said with a sardonic laugh. Mother had at one time dated Frank O'Neil, commander of our local area police headquarters in Chicago. They had remained friends, and that kind of relationship comes in handy when you find a corpse.

"I can't have one in every port, dear. Now, you wait here and I'll go call them."

"There's a phone right here."

"I know, but we probably shouldn't touch anything. I'll only be a minute."

She started out but paused in the doorway and turned back to me, "By the by, my name is Jean Robbins and you don't know me."

During our first foray into the spy business, we had not only come across assumed names, but people for whom we had no names at all. I suppose, considering what our lives had become since then, that I shouldn't have been so surprised to find my mother traveling under an alias about two thousand miles from where she was supposed to be. After a brief pause, during which I'm sure I looked as dumbfounded as I felt, I replied, "I assume you'll explain that later, too."

"Of course, dear," she said casually as she left.

While Mother went off to phone, I scanned the room. It struck me as odd that the place hadn't been tossed. Granted, there wasn't a lot here to throw around, but what little there was seemed to be in perfect order. Perhaps from having seen too many B movies, I expected this kind of murder to be accompanied by a frantic search.

The fact that the dead man was a former friend suddenly hit me, and I slumped onto the arm of the couch. "Well, Patrick," I said quietly, "now you'll never know what I wanted to say to you." Then again, I suppose he did know. But that didn't help. I had probably needed to tell him how I felt more than he'd needed to hear it, and now that would never happen.

Watching Mother give her statement was really something to behold. She fluttered and chattered as if she were Omaha's answer to Angela Lansbury. She was talking to a detective at a desk that wasn't very far from the one where I waited for the detective who was interviewing me. The room was huge and crammed with industrial desks. Everything glowed unnaturally under the overzealous, harsh fluorescent lights. It was like a nightmare version of the set for *Lou Grant*.

"I live in the building," said Mother. When I heard that I was awfully glad that my detective had crossed the room to get coffee for the two of us. I could hardly hide my astonishment.

"I haven't lived there long—I've only just moved in!" she continued, gazing wide-eyed at the detective and making a great show of being stunned by what had happened. "I certainly hope this kind of thing doesn't go on there on a regular basis. As it is, I'll probably have to move, people getting killed and such! I'll not be able to sleep, you see, not after all this."

The detective made a conciliatory grunting noise at her, then said, "Can you tell me what happened?"

43

"I have no idea what happened, but that boy who lived there, he was killed, wasn't he?"

"I mean, you were the one who called the police. How did that come about?"

"Oh, I see. Well, I heard that young man over there come in," she pointed briefly to me, and her voice had taken on a quality meant to convey that she was sure I was as pure as driven snow.

"You *heard* him come in?"

"Oh yes, you can hear every little noise in that courtyard. Every single noise. And everyone who comes into the courtyard is announced, so to speak, by the noise from the front door. It squeaks, you know, just like a knife going through your brain. I really don't see why the landlord can't do something about it. I'll certainly have to have a word with him."

She stopped and the detective stared at her blankly for a moment before saying, "Ma'am?"

"Oh!" cried Mother, looking properly embarrassed, "Oh yes . . . so I heard him come in and walk around, and I looked out my window, just to see who it was, because you can never be too careful. And I saw him walk to the dead boy's door and knock, and then he called to him, and then he tried the door." Mother's face took on a decidedly cunning look. "And then I told myself that I'd better keep watching, because I'd never seen him before and you can never be too sure if someone's just being artful about breaking in."

"Yes, ma'am."

"Anyway, he tried the door and it opened, and he had just stepped in when I suddenly heard him scream." When she said this last she looked over at me, and I got the impression that she was trying to make sure I'd heard that. I blinked.

"So I ran downstairs to see whatever was the matter," continued Mother, "and there was that poor young man dead in the bath, and that nice young boy over there looking white as a sheet as if he'd just walked in and found a dead body . . . which he had."

"I see." The detective didn't seem noticeably moved by anything Mother said, but I did get the impression that he believed her—which is not surprising. Upper-class British accents are just so eminently believable. It was also clear that he didn't make any connection between Mother and me, which I'm sure was mainly because, though Mother has scrupulously maintained her accent despite decades of living in America, I was born and raised here and my own voice has a brashness that seems to revolt against hers.

"So," said the detective, taking a deep breath, "you can hear everything, but you didn't hear a shot?"

"No, I didn't," said Mother with a disappointed shake of her head. "So you see, it must've happened last night while I was asleep."

"About what time would that be?"

"What?" said Mother, wrinkling her forehead.

"Do you remember when you went to sleep and when you got up?"

Mother sat back in her chair and looked at him as if she'd just discovered he had three arms. "Well, of course I do. I'm not daft, you know! I went to bed about eleven and got up about six."

It was at this point that Detective Rob Furness (he pronounced it "furnace" when he introduced himself) arrived back at the desk with two Styrofoam cups of coffee, one of which he handed to me.

"Thank you," I said meekly.

Furness appeared to be about forty. He was wearing a suit that looked too expensive for him and a tie with red and blue stripes that must've been a Father's Day gift. His eyes were brown and his hair was almost black, with a layer of gray that seemed to hang on the tips like frost.

He reiterated everything he'd said to me at Patrick's apartment: that they wanted me to come in with them simply so they could get a statement, not because they thought I was involved in any way. His explanation had been reassuring, but his manner had convinced me that if I resisted, I'd be thrown to the ground, cuffed, and dragged in. But that could just have been my imagination. Meeting the police at the scene of a murder has a tendency to make one feel extremely culpable. It didn't help that I'd been frisked at the scene, which the detective assured me was just a precaution.

Now he asked me how I knew the deceased (another question that he'd asked me at the scene), and I explained again that we'd gone to college together, and that I hadn't seen Patrick for almost ten years, but since I was out here with a friend on a visit I thought I'd look Patrick up.

"With a *friend*?"

I sighed. "Detective, I make no secret of being gay. Yes, with a friend. With my husband, in fact."

Furness let out a noncommittal "Hmm", then said, "This Patrick Gleason, was he gay?"

"Yes."

"So, after ten years you showed up on your friend's doorstep and found him dead?"

"Actually, I saw him for the first time yesterday. We had lunch at a place called Bixby's."

"I see." He made a note on his pad. He was silent for a couple of minutes, staring at his notes. "How was he yesterday?"

I had the distinct feeling that Furness was trying to catch me up in something, but it's possible that it was just that being a detective, he naturally looked like he suspected everybody. I said, "What do you mean?"

"Happy? Sad? Depressed? Nervous? Had he changed?"

I thought for a moment, then said, "Well, he hadn't really changed much from when I knew him."

"*Knew* him . . ."

I didn't like the way he said this. He made it sound as if all existing homosexuals would get around to having sex with each other given enough time. He also gave me the impression he was determined to make some kind of connection between my coming to L.A. and Patrick's death. Even though I knew that there couldn't conceivably be any connection, Furness's attitude was unnerving. But frankly, I could understand it if he was suspicious. Showing up just before Patrick was killed proved that I hadn't lost my impeccably bad timing.

"So he didn't give any sort of indication at this lunch of yours that anything was wrong? That he was in any danger?"

"Not at all. Just the opposite. He acted like he didn't have a care in the world."

Furness looked me directly in the eyes for a moment,

which I thought was another ploy to make me uncomfortable, so I just held his gaze, which probably made me look more guilty. God, this whole thing was making me paranoid (and that's saying a lot coming from someone who's been working for the government). At last he said, "Do you know any reason somebody'd want to kill him?"

"No, but . . ."

"Yeah?"

"I don't know how much you know about him. . . ."

Furness sat back in his chair and clasped his hands behind his neck. "Tell me."

"Well, Patrick did porno movies. Gay porn."

"Hmm." Although he took the news without emotion, I had the distinct impression that it had taken an effort for him not to raise his eyebrows.

"So I don't know if that could have anything to do with it."

"Could be," he replied very casually.

He asked me endless questions about finding the body. In fact, he asked me the same endless questions several times over, until my brain was beginning to feel like tapioca. Just when I thought I were approaching the end of my endurance, the other detective came over and showed Furness a sheet of paper that I took to be my mother's statement. Furness read it over and when he finished nodded to the detective, who went back to Mother.

"We'll have somebody drive you home, ma'am," he said.

Mother rose from her chair and glanced anxiously in my direction. She cocked her head to the side, which I took to mean that she wanted me to follow her as soon as I was able. I couldn't, by word or expression, acknowledge her for fear of the detectives taking notice, so she left without knowing whether or not I'd caught on.

"Detective Furness," I said, giving my full attention back to my interrogator, "do you really have any reason to believe I had something to do with Patrick's death?"

His eyes narrowed and he stared at me for at least thirty seconds, then he said, "As a matter of fact, no."

"You don't?"

He smiled for the first time since I'd met him. "You sound surprised."

"It's just, all these questions . . ."

His voice took on a tone that implied that my little inconvenience couldn't be helped. "Well, you didn't have a gun on you when we arrived, and according to that lady, you didn't have time to shoot this guy and then hide the gun. That kind of evidence means a lot coming from a stranger."

I felt my throat constrict.

"And I'll tell you the truth, the way he was killed—especially given the porn angle—the way he was killed looks like a hit."

"A *hit*?" I said, unable to hide my incredulity, "You mean, like, the Mob?"

"Yes, Mr. Reynolds," he said, producing an unpleasant smirk that mimicked detectives from gangster movies of the forties, "the *Mob*, organized crime."

I tried to hold my temper, but he really was trying it. "It's just that that's the type of thing you hear about, but you don't really believe it exists."

"Uh-huh."

"What makes you think it was a hit?"

He pointed to his forehead and his chest in turn, indicating where Patrick had been shot. "Head and heart. It's like a signature."

There was something curiously resigned in the way he'd uttered this brief reply that made me uneasy.

"You *do* think you can find out who did this, don't you?"

"We'll make every effort," he replied dully, sounding exactly as if that's all the effort he was prepared to make.

"You don't sound too hopeful."

"We have a lot of murders here, and the hardest ones to solve and the lowest priority are the disposables."

"Disposables?" I said, barely able to hide my contempt. "You mean like faggots?"

He glared at me. "That could hardly be the case here. I'm sure you know that some of the most important people in this town are . . . gay."

I knew that the hesitation before saying this was because at the last minute he'd thought the better of using the same word I'd used.

He continued, "I meant pushers, users, hustlers, prostitutes . . . generally the type of people that the public is glad are gone."

I stared at him blankly, because what he'd said caused me to examine myself for a moment (a reaction that I'm pretty sure Furness had been trying for). He was right: those were exactly the type of people for whom I'd never spared any sympathy when I read or heard of them being murdered. I'd go so far as to say I thought they were better off.

At last I said, "But Patrick was none of those things."

"Long time since you've seen him. A lot could've changed. And . . . one thing you should know is, a lot of those guys in gay porn are hustlers." He stopped and smirked again. " 'Scuse me. They call themselves *escorts*. It's how they make most of their money. Porn is just like advertising."

"But he was so clean," I said, sounding like a fifties housewife in an Ajax commercial.

Furness shook his head and smiled. "What do you think, hustlers are covered with soot? A street punk with scabs isn't gonna get a lot of work."

I sat there dumbly for a while. I'd thought the emotional acrobatics I'd experienced since finding Patrick on that tape had subsided after our inauspicious lunch, but on talking to this detective, they started all over again. I had, after all, once felt *something* for this man who'd been murdered, however misguided and adolescent those feelings might have been. And I couldn't accept that he'd become something so foreign to me. Betrayal is one thing, total alienation is another.

Furness broke in on my reverie by saying, "But I meant what I told you: we'll make every effort to find the killer. I just can't hold out a lot of hope to you, though."

"Sure."

My tone was unfortunate. I really didn't believe they'd do anything about Patrick's murder (and if what Furness said was true, I really didn't believe there was anything they *could* do about it), but I knew he'd meant well by saying it.

"One thing before you go, though—we'd like to take your fingerprints."

"Mine? Why?"

"Just to help in our investigation. To be able to separate yours—since we know you were there—from anybody else's."

He said this in a way that made me wonder if he was simply trying to give me grief for casting aspersions on the police, and at the same time leave me a little off balance.

"And I'd prefer that you didn't leave town for the time being."

I decided to adopt the same attitude. My eyes narrowed and I said, "Oh, I have no intention of leaving."

FIVE

Altogether I had spent several hours with the local constabulary, which is probably pretty much what one should expect when one finds an old friend shot in the bathtub. They had let me call Peter earlier, assuring me that it wasn't the proverbial "one phone call" because I wasn't under arrest. I let Peter know where I was and that I was all right, and told him everything I could, which didn't include the fact that I'd found my mother masquerading as Olympia Dukakis in Patrick's run-down apartment building. Peter didn't sound happy about any of this, but then he hadn't sounded happy since I rented that damned video.

When I left the police, I swung by the Hotel Windemere by the Sea and picked up Peter, who emerged from the hotel dressed in dark blue jeans and a sparkling white shirt with only the last three buttons done; he was wearing dark sunglasses à la Marcello Mastroianni in *8 ½*. After only a few days of California sun, his olive skin had darkened noticeably, making him even more striking, which would have been insufferable if Peter ever gave any indication that he thought himself as attractive as he is.

He jumped in the car, slid the glasses down his nose, and peered at me over the rims.

"Are you all right?"

"Except for the shock, yeah."

"What happened?"

"I have no idea," I said as I put the car in gear. "I just walked in and found him dead."

I steered out of the long semicircular drive that fronted the hotel and pulled onto Pico.

"Where are we going?" Peter asked.

"To revisit the scene of the crime."

"Why?" he asked, and I could tell his eyes were widening behind his dark glasses.

"Because there's something there you have to see."

"What?"

"You wouldn't believe me if I told you," I replied with a sigh.

I turned onto Palm Way, which seemed even more junglelike in the late afternoon sun—an impression that was helped by the sounds of unfamiliar birds and the slap of palm fronds hitting the pavement, (but I was starting to get used to that). I half expected to find toucans hopping down the street, followed closely by those cartoon natives with bones in their hair and dinner plates in their mouths.

"How did it go with the police?" Peter asked.

"Either they're not going to investigate at all, or they're only going to investigate me."

54

"You?" said Peter loudly, his pitch going up indignantly. "They think *you* could have something to do with this?"

I shook my head doubtfully. "Not really. I get the impression they're just trying to keep me off kilter, which is partly my fault. I think I might have implied that I didn't believe they were really going to investigate."

"You *might* have—"

"I couldn't help myself," I said testily. "The detective referred to Patrick as a 'disposable.' "

"Hmm," said Peter, turning to the windshield, the muscles in his face becoming taut. This had gotten to him. He wouldn't like having any human being, let alone a gay one, referred to as disposable, any more than I would.

"You think they're going to give you trouble?" he said at last.

"Oh no," I replied. "I have an absolutely unbreakable alibi, and you're about to meet her."

I found a parking space about half a block from the apartment building. The overhanging gloom of the palm trees and the afternoon heat were alleviated only by the smell of the sea. Even if you hadn't been able to smell it, you could just feel that a large body of water was nearby.

"Isn't this neighborhood *tres bleak* for a rich little porn star?" said Peter as we approached Patrick's building.

"It wasn't what I was expecting, either."

While I checked the names on the mailboxes, Peter said, "Are you sure this is wise?"

I snorted. "No, I'm sure this is really stupid, but it can't be avoided."

I located the name Robbins, which bore the number 14. We went through the broken outer door, which announced our arrival with the same rusty creak as before

55

and headed up the stairs to the second-floor landing since, on my earlier visit I'd seen only single-digit apartments on the first. Looking down from there, the circular courtyard and sad attempt at a garden looked even more feral.

"This is really lovely," said Peter, wrinkling his nose. "I must find out who does their landscaping. And what is that delightful aroma?"

"Eau de Rot," I answered flatly.

I knocked on door number 14; after a very brief pause, the door swung open.

"May I present my alibi—Mrs. Robbins, wasn't it?"

"Jean!" said Patrick. I gave him a gentle push into the apartment to help him recover from the surprise, then followed him in.

This apartment was the antithesis of Patrick's: though still not by any means sunny, it was definitely brighter, and although the furnishings weren't elaborate, they were at least clean and serviceable. The floor was covered with light brown wall-to-wall carpeting; there was a long couch with a tan slipcover, a narrow oval coffee table, and a couple of odd chairs in the living room, and a small glass table and four chairs were arranged in a dining area. It looked sort of like a lower-class hotel suite, comfortable but not the Ritz. But compared to Patrick's apartment, it was paradise.

"What are you doing here?" said Peter incredulously.

Mother motioned for us to sit on the couch. "Can I get you something to drink?"

"Explanation, Mother."

"Well, I should think it's obvious, darling. I was concerned about Patrick, just as you were, so I thought I'd come out and see if there was anything I could do."

She stopped speaking and folded her hands in her lap, her expression clearly implying that she thought she'd said enough. Peter and I continued to stare at her.

"And?" I said at last.

"And . . . that's all. That's why I'm here. Isn't that why *you're* here?"

I sighed. "Mother, the day after we came out here, you told me on the phone that you couldn't locate Patrick. Three days later we find you living in his apartment building. Don't you think that calls for a bit more explanation? In the first place, how in the hell did you find him? And how did you get an apartment in his building? And why didn't you tell me what you were doing?"

"Your first two questions can be answered with three words—"

"Agent Lawrence Nelson," Peter interjected, a smile growing across his face.

"Exactly. The day after you called, it suddenly occurred to me that the easiest way to track someone down was by using our . . . private associates. It really was so thick of us not to have thought of it in the first place. Since you were pretty sure Patrick was out here, all I had to do was call our 'boss' at the CIA and ask him if he could locate him. It took about an hour." She turned to Peter and said, "Those people seem to know everything. It's really quite disheartening."

I slapped my forehead. "Oh God, why didn't I think of that? Do you know how much time I could've saved?"

"Quite."

"And Nelson arranged for the apartment?"

"Well, that's the odd part. When he called me back with Patrick's address and phone, he did the most peculiar thing."

She stopped again, this time as a shameless plea for prompting. I said with irritation, "What?"

"First, he asked me why I'd wanted to know about Patrick, and I explained. Then, he asked me what I intended to do, and I told him I really just thought I might want to talk to Patrick. I didn't tell him that the two of you were already out here, and I didn't think it necessary to go into that pornography business with Nelson. After all, on a need-to-know basis, he didn't need to know."

She said this last part with a coy gleam in her eye that would've made me laugh out loud if I hadn't still been so perplexed by her presence. In her own humble way, she was simply seizing the opportunity of repaying Nelson for the times he'd made us work in the dark.

"So what was peculiar?" Peter asked.

"I'm getting to that," said Mother. "He asked me if he could arrange for me to have an apartment in this building, would I consider staying here."

Peter and I glanced at each other, and his face looked just the way mine felt. We turned back to Mother.

"Why would he do that?"

"I don't know," she said with a shrug. "And I'm not sure I want to know."

I could sympathize. After our previous dealings with Nelson, I'd come to believe that sometimes it was better to not know things, even on a need-to-know basis.

"Didn't you ask him why?" said Peter.

"Of course I did. As usual, he didn't give me much of an explanation, but he said it was to my benefit. He said that it might give me a chance to watch your friend a little while before I decided how to approach him."

"In other words, Nelson never said why it would benefit *him* if you would stay here."

"Exactly. All he asked me to do was hold off a few days before approaching Patrick, and to keep my eyes and ears open and let him know if anything unusual happened." Her brow furrowed, as if a thought had suddenly struck her. "I suppose I'll have to call him, now that Patrick's been killed. I suppose that's unusual."

"But you knew I wanted to talk to him myself," I said, my voice approaching a whine.

She shot a quick, involuntary glance at Peter and said, "I know. But I didn't know whether or not that was wise, all things considered."

"You should have told me you'd found him. You could've saved me a lot of time and trouble."

Mother sighed and her face became much more serious. "I probably should have, darling, but I knew you'd want to rush over here with me, or ahead of me, or without me, and I thought I might be able to do more good on my own."

"God," I said, "you really *are* my mother, aren't you?"

"Well, sometimes running into an old friend's mother can shake you up more than running into an old friend."

"There you have me. I have a feeling that if I ran into somebody's mother while I was making porno movies I'd feel pretty naked." Both Peter and Mother stared at me incredulously. I added, "You know what I mean."

"I thought maybe I could talk some sense into him," continued Mother. "As it turned out, I never got the chance."

"Weren't you afraid he'd recognize you?" Peter asked.

"Not in that hat," I said wryly. "You didn't see how she was done up this morning. She really did look like she'd just come in from pruning the wisteria. She was swathed in hats and material. . . ."

"I was flowing," said Mother.

"It was a minute before *I* recognized her."

"I'm not sure he would've recognized me, anyway. I don't think I saw him more than a couple of times, even though he and Alex were friends. Patrick wasn't the type who took notice of one's family."

No, I thought sardonically, *a trick usually doesn't.*

"And besides, you have to remember, I was under orders to lie low. I wasn't supposed to let him get a good look at me, I don't think. At least not for a few days."

Peter clucked his tongue. "This is a pretty bizarre arrangement, even for Nelson."

"Oh, I don't know," said Mother with a fanciful wave of her hand, "I don't know what he's on about, but I didn't see what harm there was in going along with him. Actually, I thought it might be good to get the lay of the land before speaking to Patrick. After all, we have no way of knowing if that tape you saw him in was just an aberration, or if that's really how he was making his living."

"That's how he was doing it, all right. I had lunch with him yesterday."

"Really? Oh, dear."

"I have one other question," I said.

"Hmm?"

"Why in the hell did you call yourself Mrs. Robbins? Why didn't you just use your own name?"

"Oh," she said waving it off, "that was just a lark!"

This is the woman who raised me.

"*Did* you see anything unusual this past week?" asked Peter.

"Only my son arriving and finding a dead body," she replied, "and the usual comings and goings. I have a wonderful view for it, too. Come and see."

As she led us to the kitchen window she said, "The garden's a fright."

The kitchen window sported light yellow curtains bespeckled with tiny white flowers—an addition to the apartment for which I felt sure Mother was responsible. She pulled back one side of the curtains, and the three of us peered out. There was a very clear, slightly aerial view of Patrick's apartment directly across the courtyard on the first floor. Yellow-and-black police tape was strung in a zigzag pattern across his door. It somehow didn't look entirely out of place in this setting.

"That's a very interesting view," said Peter as we drew back into the living room. "it makes you wonder, doesn't it?"

"What?" I said.

"Whether or not that's what Nelson wanted her to watch."

"Exactly," said Mother, "but he didn't tell me what to look for. He just told me to look for anything unusual."

"And you didn't get to talk to Patrick at all?"

She shook her head. "Remember, I only just arrived day before yesterday, and I was lying low. He wasn't here all that much—he was in and out. He only had one visitor since then. A young man. Very nice looking."

"I don't doubt it," I said.

At this point we heard the bang of the outer door, and a pair of sandals slapped noisily into the courtyard. The

61

three of us crossed back to the window in unison and peered out. A young man strode into view and came to an abrupt halt when he saw the yellow-and-black tape. The last echo of his slapping sandals stopped a brief second after the man did, as if it had been choked by the foliage. He stood immobile for a moment. He was wearing white Onionskin shorts through which a thong was clearly evident, and he carried a black sports bag over his shoulder. His shirt was wrapped around the strap.

I stepped out onto the balcony and said, "Excuse me, are you here to see Patrick?"

He did a double-take, then looked up at me, shielding his eyes. "Yeah?" He sounded uncertain.

"Um . . . I'm a friend of his. Something's happened. Come on up."

He hesitated for a moment, then said, "Sure," and started around to the stairs.

I watched him as he came up. Though I refer to him as a man, I don't think he could have been a minute over nineteen. He was really quite a specimen: smallish but well built; perfectly oval head, large brown eyes, and short dark brown hair cut like Julius Caesar's. He was in incredibly good shape, obviously through a regular exercise regimen. The muscles of his legs bulged, his chest was chiseled, and he had one of those washboard stomachs that I always think look painful. His overtly masculine physique starkly contrasted the boyishness of his face.

"Come on in," I said, "my mother and my husband are here."

He paused again with the hesitation of someone who through a lifetime of unpleasant surprises has learned not to trust anyone. "That's okay," he said, which I took to mean that he saw no reason to go into any enclosed space with strangers. He dropped his bag to the ground, unwrapped his shirt, and slipped it on. It was light blue and had a pair of pink palm trees printed on the left breast.

"What's happened? Where's Pat?"

"Are you a friend of his?"

" 'Course. That's why I'm here."

He had a slight, limp-wristed lisp that was out of sync with his muscles. He wouldn've sounded like he was doing a parody of a faggot, if only it hadn't been so consistent.

"Who are you?" he added, his tone implying he didn't necessarily think I had any right to ask him anything.

"Oh, I'm an old friend of Pat's—I'm just here for a visit. My name's Alex."

"Jeff Durkin," he said. He glanced down at the taped apartment door and said, "So what's happened? Where's Pat?"

"Well . . . I hate to tell you this, but he's dead. He was shot last night."

His brown eyes widened the way Ricky Ricardo's did before exploding at Lucy, but all he said was "Jesus . . ."—which came out something like "Jethus"—"Jesus Jesus Jesus . . ."

His legs wobbled and he started to sink to the ground. I grabbed his arm and yelled "Wait!" stupidly, as if he could pause in his fainting while I got him a pillow. Then I turned to the open apartment door and yelled "Mother!"

Jeff didn't become totally unconscious; he just seemed to momentarily lapse into a dazed, rubbery state. Peter and I each hooked an arm under his and half carried or half dragged him to the dining table. His legs tried to help a lit-

63

tle but didn't seem to be able to get a good grip on the floor.

We dropped him into a chair and I retrieved his sports bag and set it by his side. I left the door to the apartment wide open so as not to throw the poor guy into an additional panic. I sat across from him silently and Peter stood by his side with a calming hand on his shoulder while Mother got him a cup of tea. She always insisted with a typically British tinge of wry humor that hot tea was a good restorative even in hot weather, because it equalized your body temperature. I contend that only the sheer strength of her conviction could make that one work.

Jeff's head lolled a bit to the side as if he was having trouble keeping it balanced on his neck, and his eyes looked wide and unfocused, like those Mexican children painted on black velvet. When Mother put the tea in front of him, he almost instantly seemed to regain some of his composure. Peter took a seat to my left, while Mother hung back in the kitchen, apparently sensing that this particular young man would be more forthcoming without a mother's presence.

He ran his palm across his forehead. "I'm sorry," he said, the faint lisp making him sound fragile, "I don't think I've ever done that before."

"It was pretty bad news," I said.

"You say he was shot? When did it happen? Last night?"

"Yes."

His eyes grew even wider, "Wow. Then I must've been the last guy he fucked." He took another sip of tea.

From the doorway to the kitchen, Mother shot me a glance that seemed to say, "If you're *ever* in the position of saying that, I hope to God you've completely fallen out of contact with me."

"You were with him last night?" I asked.

He looked at each of us in turn, and there was a doe-in-the-headlights quality about his expression that made him look more startled than I thought he should have been.

Sensing his confusion, Peter said, "What Alex means is, were you filming last night?"

Jeff looked relieved. Then he glanced from Peter to me, and his face reddened. Surprisingly enough, he looked genuinely embarrassed.

"You know about the videos then, right?" he said, evidently unaware that if we hadn't known, he'd just given it away.

I nodded. "Yeah."

Jeff shifted in his chair. He lifted the cup to his lips and took a gulp of tea, which had by now cooled off a bit. A little of the liquid trickled from the corner of his mouth and continued down his jaw. He wiped it away with the back of his hand. There was something unconsciously sensual about the way he did this, as if he'd been programmed from birth in how to turn his elders on, and now did it as a matter of course. Naturally. Like a sexual Manchurian Candidate.

He said, "Yeah, we worked together yesterday, but it was afternoon, not night."

"Where did you work?" I asked.

"At a house. Just some guy's house . . . by the pool."

Peter asked, "Did Patrick happen to say what he was going to be doing last night?"

65

"Not to me, but I was up first, and I didn't hang around after."

"Sorry?" I said.

"I just had one scene: Pat topped me and then I did a cum shot. That was all." He delivered this as if he were rattling off a recipe for spaghetti. " 'Course it took forever, with all those fucking angles."

Peter rolled his eyes at me while Jeff took another deep gulp of tea. I preferred to assume that Jeff had been referring to the camera.

"Patrick didn't leave when you did?"

"Naw. He was gonna do another guy, so he stayed and I split. I guess he was there for a while after."

"Then you weren't the last guy to . . ." I thought for a moment, not wanting to use Jeff's word. "Then you weren't the last guy to 'be with' him."

He stared at me for a moment, then looked incredibly relieved. "Yeah, he fucked somebody else last."

It crossed my mind how many people Patrick had done that to in a variety of ways. It wasn't a pleasant thought that the end of his life would be marked by who he'd done it to last.

Jeff glanced from Peter to me again, blinking his long lashes a couple of times. "Why the questions? You're not the cops, are you?"

"No. We . . . I mean, Patrick was an old friend of mine, and I saw him for the first time in years just yesterday. Like you said, it was a shock to find him dead this morning. I'm just interested in what was going on with him."

"Well," he said, pausing to drink a little more, "I can't really help ya with that. I just met him yesterday."

"You just met him yesterday . . ." I began incredulously. My forehead creased like a pair of linen pants. I'd been about to say ". . . and you had sex with him?" but thought the better of it just in time. It's amazing how quickly your middle-class upbringing will come flying out of you at the most inappropriate times. I'd apparently gotten over my shock at Patrick fucking for a living enough to be shocked at the idea that he would be fucking somebody he didn't know. There's something distinctly Catholic about that kind of reasoning.

"If you didn't know him, what were you doing coming here today?" I asked.

He smiled sheepishly and shook his hand as if waving off the matter of no importance. "We made a date to go to the gym together. He was in pretty good shape, but he wanted to work at it more."

My tongue involuntarily clucked against the roof of my mouth. I could feel the lines deepening across my forehead. "You made a date to go to the gym while the two of you were . . ."

"Uh-huh." He nodded, his eyes pointed in my direction, staring blankly as if a horn had just sprouted from my head. I suddenly had the sensation that somewhere after passing thirty I had become irrevocably provincial, and I was trying to remember the exact moment it happened.

"Do any of you guys—the ones that do the videos—know each other personally?" The question seemed bizarre even to me.

" 'Course we do. Sure. Couldn't help it. Like, I know Ted—he's the one that got me my first job. I don't know a lot of them 'cause I haven't been doing it too long. 'Spose I'll get to know most of them here if I keep it up."

Peter and I exchanged glances, but I looked away quickly, fearing one of us might laugh.

"You see," I said, clearing my throat, "we'd like to get hold of some of Patrick's friends. We'd like to meet them."

"We would?" said Peter.

I nodded at him. "Do you know anybody who knew him . . . better than you did?"

"No, but I'll bet somebody does."

Peter and I once again glanced at each other. I was wondering if anyone could be quite as dense as this guy appeared to be. I said as gently as possible, "Well, of course *somebody* does. The question is do you know who?"

"No, I mean one of the other guys. Ol' Pat's been in the business for a while. At least I think he was. He sure fucked like it."

"He was in *that* business for more than a while," said Peter under his breath. It was the first indication I'd gotten of how angry he was on my behalf.

"Where can we start?" I said, hoping Jeff could give us a few names.

He thought for a minute, sucking in his lower lip. I'd hate to sound like I was looking down on anyone, but he really looked . . . not quite intelligent. After a long pause he said, "Well, we're gonna have a pretty-party tonight."

"A what?"

"That's what we call it, but what it is, is one of the producers is throwing a party, and most of the guys that'll be there are in the business. Pretty, see? There's sure to be somebody there that knew Patrick better than I did."

"Who's giving this one?"

"Mano Man Productions. They're the only one I've worked for, so far."

"Do you think it'd be all right if we went?"

Jeff glanced from one to the other of us, then said, "I think you'd pass."

I didn't *even* want to pursue that.

"You can say you're friends of mine. You won't have any trouble if you do that."

"By the way," I said as an afterthought, "Do you know who it was that Patrick was going to be 'acting' with after you?" I couldn't help apostrophizing the word, but Jeff didn't seem to notice.

"Sure. It was Brett Lover."

"I don't suppose you know his real name?" asked Peter.

Jeff looked disappointed when he admitted that he didn't, and that he hadn't gotten to meet Lover, in a professional sense or otherwise. "He's a star. I hope I get to meet him tonight. He's beautiful. He'll probably be at the party. He's my idol."

I suppose if none of the Kennedys are available . . .

We listened as Jeff's sandals slapped their way to the door and out of the apartment building. He had left behind directions to the party as well as his own address and phone number in case we wanted to get hold of him. His eyes held mine just a little too long when he said this, an implied invitation that I was in no hurry to clarify. When the door slammed behind him, it echoed in the empty courtyard like the lid falling back to earth and resealing the Ark of the Covenant in *Raiders of the Lost Ark*. It was a dead, empty sound that accentuated the way I felt at that moment.

"What a sorry young man," said Mother as she and Peter crossed into the living room.

"Yeah," said Peter.

Mother stopped in the act of taking a seat on the couch and looked at me. I was still staring out the kitchen window at the depressing scene in which Patrick had lived his so-called high life and met his death. I realized that within days, probably within hours, the tape would be gone, along with the scraps of furniture, and someone else would move in. All memory of Patrick would be completely wiped away.

"What's up with you, Alex?" said Mother.

"I was just thinking . . . that I was too late to help Patrick."

"If it comes to that," said Peter gently, "it was years too late. He didn't grow into this situation overnight."

"Darling"—Mother crossed to me and put her hands on my shoulders—"you don't even know that what happened to him had anything to do with those videos. It could have been anything. He could have surprised a burglar or something."

"Here?" I said, pointing out to the courtyard.

"Well, maybe not a burglar. But it could have been any number of things."

"You don't believe that," I said, pulling away from her. I went into the living room and dropped dejectedly on the couch. "And neither do the police. They think it was some kind of hit."

"Look, babe," said Peter, sitting beside me and taking my hand, "even if his death had something to do with the videos, you're not responsible. Doing what he did was his choice. He told you that much himself. There isn't anything else you could have done."

"He's right, you know," Mother added.

For the first time in my life, I knew what they mean when they describe someone as vacant. It was as if all my emotions had packed up and moved out, leaving behind some confusing, mismatched luggage. And I felt a vague sense of anger, like a landlord who finds a tenant has left some heavy belongings behind. Peter squeezed my hand more tightly, and Mother sat on my other side, gently laying an arm across my shoulders.

"I know one thing. I want to find out who killed him."

"The police are going to do that, Alex," said Mother firmly.

"The police consider Patrick disposable, Mother."

She stared blankly at me for a moment.

"Did *they* say that?" she asked with indignation.

I nodded.

Her expression hardened and the corners of her mouth sloped downward as the meaning of the words sank in. I hadn't had time to tell her what the detective's attitude had been when I was questioned, but her reaction told me that she was less happy about it than I was. We sat together silently for a few minutes; then Mother said, "Maybe we *should* look into this." After a moment added, "But I don't know where we'll start. After all, we're not detectives, we're spies."

But Peter and I knew where to start: the pretty-party.

SIX

We tried to urge Mother to move into the Hotel Windemere by the Sea along with us, but she would have none of it. She thought it just possible she might be able to find out something for herself if she remained in Patrick's building.

"I'm sure the murder will be the talk of the building. I'm bound to be able to pick up some information."

"You know, I think I'm legitimately worried about your safety," I protested.

"Why? There's no reason to connect me to anybody or anything here."

"*Yet*," I said. "That could change if you're too obvious in your snooping."

Mother bristled, then replied in her most prim British accent, "It would appear, darling, that it's only 'snooping' when it's done in the third person. In the first person, it's 'investigating.' "

I was suitably abashed. I blushed so hotly I thought my hair might burn off.

Peter and I returned to our hotel to freshen up and get some rest before the party. I took a long bath that lulled me into the kind of repose from which it is very difficult to rise. When I was finally able to pull myself out, Peter took a shower and then we adjourned for cocktails on the balcony. We were wet and warm, mellow from the water and even more mellow from the drinks. A sultry wind stirred the hem of Peter's paisley-print silk robe, giving me brief glimpses of the equipment with which I was so familiar. The years hadn't diminished his ability to stimulate me. I smiled and took a sip of my rum and Coke. As we sat there looking out at the water through the early evening haze, the combination of the alcohol and the heat made me feel civilized and respectable and sexy all at the same time. I would have much preferred to stay there for the evening and bask in the warmth of my husband, but we had work that couldn't be avoided.

The cocktails had been accompanied by our room service order of salads and warm bread, on which we dined before getting ready for the evening.

"What exactly do you wear to a 'pretty-party'?" said Peter, curling his lips around the last two words with distaste.

"I'd imagine it depends on how pretty you want to be."

Peter opted for a fresh white shirt and a pair of black denim pants that were a little on the tight side, to my way of thinking, since we were going into a den of iniquity. When I pointed this out, he had the gall to say, "You catch more flies with honey, honey," with a glint in his eye that made me think he just might be getting back at me for something. I wore jeans and a baby-blue, long-tailed gauze shirt that makes my eyes look bluer than they really are. We both wore sandals and chose to forgo underwear in honor of our descent into hell.

Jeff had told us that the party would be kicking off around seven-thirty, so we waited until nine o'clock before we left the hotel, figuring that we'd be less conspicuous if the party was in full swing when we arrived. We got on Pacific Coast Highway and headed for Malibu. The drive seemed longer than it was because of my unfamiliarity with the road, which was dark despite the sporadic streetlights. Jeff hadn't known the address of the house, but was able to give us such detailed directions that it made me suspect he'd been memorizing the route just in case he'd have to describe it to the police later.

We located the turn he'd indicated. The road curved up something I would have called a cliff and we took a left as instructed at the top on a street called Small Rock. Jeff had told us that the house would be easy to spot, because it was the third one in from the turn and was what he called a "Frank Lloyd Wrong," a joke I was pretty sure he was repeating without knowing what it meant.

Small Rock was long and dark, with very few houses. The street was lined with cars. The party house would have been easy to spot even without the description: every light in the building was on, and the sounds of music, splashing, and general carrying on could be heard clearly over the roar of the surf. The other houses were tastefully lighted in a way that probably meant the owners were out for the evening.

We parked on a steep incline quite a distance from the house. I said a silent prayer that the rental car's emergency brakes would hold. We got out of the car and looked at each other across the roof. Peter said, "Yea, though I walk through the valley of the shadow of death . . ."

"Shut up." I replied.

Two or three other cars were cruising slowly down the street, apparently looking for parking spaces. As we walked through the darkness to the house, my hand stole into Peter's. I don't know if it was because this marked the beginning of a potentially dangerous investigation, or because of my innate fear of facing a crowd of faggots that I don't know. I suspect it was more the latter, because I felt like I was about to enter a particularly rowdy gay bar, something that I would avoid like the plague under any normal circumstances, especially after what happened to me the last time I was in one.*

"So what are we going to say at the door?" asked Peter.

"Just what Jeff told us to say: that we're friends of his. He said we wouldn't have any trouble getting in."

Whoever had originally dubbed the house a Frank Lloyd Wrong had been accurate: it looked like it'd been designed by somebody who was familiar with Wright's designs, but didn't have the expertise or imagination to carry it off. The straight, jutting lines so common to Wright were attempted through having the flat roof extend a foot or more over the sides of the house, but the effect was more as if someone had dropped an absurdly oversized board across a cracker box. The front door stood open, and was

*See *Government Gay.*

guarded by a very large musclebound man wearing black leather pants and no shirt. He had a gun in a shoulder holster that was pulled tightly into his skin. His head, armpits, and torso were clean shaven.

"This isn't a leather party, is it?" I whispered to Peter. I'm afraid leather queens give me the willies.

"Who the hell knows?"

As we approached the door, the man held up a palm to stop us. There was a studded leather strap around his wrist.

"Invited?"

I looked at Peter. This really was something like what I expected the gate to hell to be like, but that wasn't the question I'd expect to be asked.

I looked back at the man and said, "We're friends of Jeff Durkin. He invited us."

He lowered his arm.

"Names?"

I told him our names and he wrote them on a clipboard.

"Go," he said, extending his arm through the doorway.

We walked past him and he turned back to the darkness to greet the next arrivals. I whispered to Peter, "I feel just like Julie Andrews in *S.O.B.*"

The room that we walked into was what I'd have thought of as a Californian nightmare: there was glass everywhere. The west wall seemed to consist entirely of a window that looked out over the ocean. There were delicate objets d'art everywhere, on occasional tables and pedestals and in showcases, as if *daring* an earthquake to touch them.

A long narrow deck stretched across the outside of the

front windows. There were a few men there, draped along the railing, smoking and sipping cocktails. It looked like a scene from *Now, Voyager.*

"There's an awful lot of noise for so few people," said Peter.

We stepped through the sliding doors onto the deck, and though no heads turned in our direction I had the feeling that everyone there had glanced at us and immediately sized us up: exactly like in a gay bar. Once outside, we could see that the deck continued along to the side of the house, and the bulk of the party appeared to be going on there, hidden from direct view.

We followed the deck around the corner and thought we'd walked into a Roman orgy. The deck swung out into a huge wooden patio on which was a veritable sea of men in all stages of dress and undress, everything from tuxedos to pubic hair, conservative coifs to pierced navels and nipples: the very type of variety that's supposed to make the gay world so diverse, and usually just manages to make me nervous.

Speakers mounted at the corners of the eaves were blaring out "Walk Like an Egyptian." Several of the men were trying to do just that, and sported the eye makeup and loincloths to prove it. It made me smile to hear the Bangles again, and reminded me of one thing I love about my brothers and sisters in gayness: always at the forefront of fashion and never afraid to be retro. In the center of the deck was a large lighted pool reminiscent of the bath in *Spartacus,* in which several naked men of the lifeguard variety were swimming leisurely laps. Japanese lanterns were strung around the perimeter of the patio in an obvious attempt at kitsch.

There were three or four men (I was never quite sure how many, because they were circulating around the periphery of the party) dressed in pseudo police garb. At first I thought they were just further examples of the colorful variety of guests, but I noticed that they were packing none-too-discreet guns, so I took it that they were there to make sure that things didn't get too far out of hand. I couldn't imagine what kind of boundaries this event had.

The guests all appeared to be having a good time, as if, despite the wretched excess, the noise, and the nudity, this was nothing more than good clean fun. At least that's what I thought until a boy who looked no older than fifteen flounced in our direction. He was clad in a short toga, which exposed one sunken nipple. He didn't look clean shaven; he looked as if he hadn't begun to develop facial hair yet. He proffered a shallow bowl full of pills and said, "Have one. It'll really loosen your pucker-hole."

My butt clenched and I said primly, "Mine is quite loose enough, thank you."

After the boy had swung away in another direction, Peter turned to me and said, sotto voce, "Jesus Christ, we've landed on the planet *Satyricon*."

I chalk it up to the years we'd been together that he'd read my mind. Like most of our brethren, Peter and I live your basic, typical, respectable middle-class lives. All of our gay friends are in committed relationships and have been for years, as are most of our straight friends. This type of gay-subculture soirée is about as foreign to us as a bestiality luau would be to a fundamentalist Christian. And just as unnerving.

The music segued into another Bangles hit, "Eternal Flame," and several of the men paired off for a slow dance.

We made our way around the pool to the bar, for which the host, whose identity we'd not yet discovered, had hired a suitably attractive bartender. He was wearing black pants and a red bow tie over a ruffled tuxedo shirtfront, without the rest of the shirt. He had light brown hair, dark blue eyes, and teeth that seemed to sparkle in the moonlight.

"What'll it be, boys?"

"Two rum and Cokes," said Peter.

The bartender sloshed the liquids into glasses with the sloppiness of a seasoned pro, and handed them to each of us in turn with a little wink. We crossed the remainder of the deck, ending up by the wooden railing on the far side, slid up onto it and sat. From this vantage point we could view most of the action, and since nobody seemed to be paying any particular attention to us, we used the opportunity to survey the partygoers. I don't know what I'd expected, but I was relieved that there was no overt sex going on. However, I had the uncomfortable feeling that if anyone shouted "action," I'd find myself in a scene from *Caligula*.

Despite everything, it seemed to be progressing like a normal party. People were standing and talking in various cliquish groups. The only difference here being the rather bizarre disparity of dress. In one group, an extremely striking man in a tuxedo was casually discussing something with a man who was dressed (as near as I could tell) as Nefertiti. In another group three men dressed in white shirts and pastel pants, a sort of post–*Miami Vice* casual, were talking to another man who was wearing a G-string as if they were carrying on a normal business meeting. For all I knew they could have been doing just that.

A hulking, athletic young man lifted himself out of the pool near where we were standing. He was naked, and strutting with the bravado of someone who's trying to convince you he's comfortable. He walked over to us, smoothing back his dripping hair.

"Hi."

"Hello," I said with that "Where do I look?" feeling that I get when someone greets me in the locker room at the health club.

He sniffed a couple of times and said, "Do you guys know anybody here?"

"Not really," said Peter.

The man shrugged, said, "Neither do I," and dove back into the pool.

I took a sip of my drink and said to Peter, "You know, I've never thought of myself as conservative, but these people are making me feel like a Republican."

It must have been the superfluity of movement that made one man in particular catch my eye, because he was almost still. He was sitting directly across the pool from us on a lounge chair. He had a head of very long, unruly black hair, and a bushy black beard, as well as a thick coat of dark body hair, visible since he was only wearing swimming trunks. There was a drink sitting on the left arm of the chair, and in his right hand he held a cigar from which he took a puff just often enough to keep it lit. It was the only movement he exhibited. Even though he was wearing very dark sunglasses (which was odd in itself, since it was night) I had the sense that his eyes were on the move. And I had the even more uncomfortable feeling that they'd shifted in our direction more than once. The party seemed to be slowly whirling around him. I cleared my throat to get Peter's attention and directed him to the ape-man with what I hoped was a discreet nod.

"Not one of the actors," said Peter.

Before I could respond I heard a slightly familiar voice say, "Hi!"

Jeff Durkin had appeared at our side without our hearing his approach, which wasn't surprising, with all the noise. But it was disconcerting just the same. He wore a dark blue thong and nothing else. I suppose that dressing for this party for him had merely amounted to slipping out of his Onionskins. I'd be lying if I said I didn't notice that he really did have the body of a Greek god, even if it was a shortish one. His cherubic face still seemed out of place on that masculine torso. He was carrying a full champagne glass in his right hand, and he sipped at it repeatedly as if it were a nervous habit.

"Whad'ya think?" he said.

"It doesn't leave much to the imagination," I replied.

He made a smacking sound and smiled. "I mean about the party."

"It doesn't leave much to the imagination."

He laughed a little too quickly and loudly, and I thought he just might have partaken of the bowl of pills being circulated by the vassal.

God, I thought, *you're so young!*

I had the nagging feeling that I was going to want to save him—despite the fact that I'd already failed with Patrick. Or maybe because of it.

"So how's it going? Have you found any of Patrick's friends?"

"We just got here," said Peter. "We haven't had much of a chance to meet anybody." I couldn't help catching his doubtful tone. He sounded as if he thought it preferable to remain unacquainted with our fellow guests.

"Well, Brett Lover's here. I've seen him," said Jeff, starting to gyrate in time to the music. "Isn't this great?"

I didn't respond right away, I was so agog at the surroundings.

"Isn't it?" Jeff repeated with the wide-eyed urgency of a teenager who desperately needs his opinions validated.

"It reminds me of the 'Poor Jenny' number in *Star!*"

"Huh?"

There is absolutely nothing that can make you feel older more quickly than that one syllable.

"A Julie Andrews movie. For some reason our foray into this fag bash keeps bringing Dame Julie to mind."

"Oh, yeah, right," replied Jeff in a distant way that verified that he had no idea what I was talking about. I sincerely hoped it was *Star!* he'd never heard of, and not Julie Andrews. But I wasn't about to press my luck.

"God, look at that guy," said Jeff, pointing at one of the pool bunnies. "It's like bein' in a candy store! Look at them!"

There were now about a half-dozen men swimming languidly back and forth. I almost expected Esther Williams to rise from the center of the pool wearing nothing but a crown of sparklers and a smile.

"What are they doing?" I said.

Jeff looked at me as if I were a bit slow. "Auditioning."

I fought the urge to cluck my tongue, which I knew would make me sound even older. Instead, I said, "Do you know a lot of the people here?"

"Only the ones I've fucked—I mean, acted with. Some of the others, I've seen some of their videos, but I don't know them. And there's some directors here, I think, and some producers. Least, that's what I heard."

"But you don't know if any of them were friends of Patrick's."

"Uh-uh," he said easily, "like I told you, I don't know any of his friends."

I glanced at Peter. This was going to be harder than we thought. We couldn't very well go around asking these people if they'd known Patrick without drawing attention to ourselves. And I was afraid we'd already done that with at least one person.

"Jeff," I said cautiously, not wanting to attract the further notice of the man on the lounge chair, "do you know who that man is?"

"Which one?"

"The hairy one, across the pool."

He started to rotate his ass seductively in time to the music. He made no effort to disguise the fact that he was peering across the pool. The ape-man had been joined by a man in a dark gray suit, who now crouched beside the deck chair and was talking to the ape quietly but intensely. The suit looked out of place because it was too middle-of-the-road; everyone else was either overdressed or underdressed. The suit just said business. I wondered what he could have to do with the ape.

"Oh," said Jeff, his voice going up an octave, " 'Course, sure! That's Derrick."

"Derrick?"

"Derrick Holmes. This is his place. He directed the video that me and Pat did yesterday. Hi, Derrick!"

Jeff waved happily. I'm not sure, but I think Holmes's head moved very slightly, and he flicked a cigar ash in Jeff's direction.

"So that guy is the director for Mano Man Productions?" asked Peter.

"He *is* Mano Man Productions," Jeff replied with childlike awe. "He's the producer and the director."

"You mean nobody else works for the company? I mean, besides the actors?"

"Sure. There's a guy that does the camera. I mean, Derrick tells him what he wants, that's how much in control he is. Ren Forrest, he's the cameraman. That guy over there."

Jeff pointed out an unremarkable man who sat alone on a stool by the side of the house.

"Is this where you filmed?"

Jeff finally stopped gyrating and looked out around the patio as if he was searching for something. He bit the nail of his index finger absently. "Actually, we did it over there," he said, pointing at the opposite corner of the pool. "Derrick usually uses his own place. And I think he has a warehouse he uses somewhere."

Peter said, "Could you point Brett Lover out to us?"

The music changed again, this time to Gloria Gaynor and "I Will Survive" (which I found unfortunately hopeful under the circumstances) as Jeff surveyed the crowd. The pseudo-Egyptians started a line dance.

"There he is," said Jeff, pointing to a pair of men talking by the bar. One was tall and blond and dressed in a tuxedo; the other seemed much younger, was wearing a jock sock, and had a bull's-eye painted on his ass.

"Which one?" said Peter.

"The one in the tux."

Both Peter and I breathed a sigh of relief. It was proof

of the old adage that clothes make the man that we both believed that a man in a tuxedo would probably be more intelligent than a human dartboard.

"Oh, look! Derrick's free."

I glanced across the pool and saw that Jeff was right: the man in the gray suit had disappeared.

"I gotta go over and make nice with him," said Jeff. "I could use the work. He's only used me once."

With this he proceeded to dance his way slowly around the pool, apparently savvy enough to make his route a little circuitous so that his intentions wouldn't be obvious. I had the feeling that the director was smart enough to see through the ruse.

"Used once, but it lasts a lifetime," said Peter solemnly.

We watched as Lover said something to his companion, then left the bar for an isolated space by the railing. He leaned up against it in a pose lifted directly from the International Male catalogue.

He was taller than most of the people there, and very slender. He had a thin Germanic face, sharp blue eyes, pointed nose, and a small mouth with disproportionately thick lips. On him this wasn't a flaw. If anything, it made him look exotic. His hair was parted in the middle and there was a pair of round glasses poised on his nose. His bearing, coupled with his looks and the tuxedo, made him look as if he should be attending the Academy Awards rather than a debauch.

As we approached, he turned toward us with an expression that said he was receiving.

"Hi," I said lamely, "I'm Alex and this is Peter."

"Um-hm," he said, pulling a cigarette from the inner pocket of his jacket.

"Can we talk to you a minute?"

He lit the cigarette and said, "Video or escort?"

"I beg your pardon?"

"I have to tell you ahead of time . . ." He paused dramatically to take a pull at the cigarette. Without tilting his head he blew a stream of smoke over my head. "If it's a video, I'm very selective. I don't work with cheesy companies." He looked down his nose at me, as if he was sure that I made nudie movies in public bathrooms with an eight-millimeter camera.

"We don't make videos," I said.

He brightened a little, a smirk playing about his lips as he glanced at Peter, then turned back to me. "You need an escort? For the two of you?"

In another of my all-too-frequent lapses of intelligence, before I could stop myself I said, "Why would the two of us need an escort?"

Peter rolled his eyes. Lover made a great show of stifling a laugh, his right hand gliding up to his mouth as his shoulders slid up and down a couple of times.

Peter cut in, "No, we don't need an escort; we just wanted to talk to you."

"You're not *fans*, are you?" he said, emphasizing the word with distaste.

"Actually, I don't think we've ever seen you before," said Peter with a malicious twinkle in his eye.

"We're friends of Patrick Gleason," I added quickly, hoping to distract him from Peter's tone.

"Oh, Pat, yeah," he replied with disinterest.

"You know he's been killed?"

"Really," he said without inflection. His eyebrows slid up a little. It was an action that made me sure he'd already heard about the murder, because I had to believe that no matter how thick his veneer, news that someone he'd had sex with the day before had been murdered couldn't help but get more of a reaction.

I nodded. "Just last night, and . . . we were hoping we could talk to you about him."

"Why?" said Lover, sticking the cigarette back between his lips and inhaling.

I glanced at Peter. "We understood that you knew him."

"We fucked a few times. I wouldn't say we were friends." He exhaled the smoke across the top of my hair.

"Well, he was a friend of mine, and I really need to talk to somebody else that knew him."

"You gotta know somebody who knew him better than I did."

I hesitated. "Not recently. You see, we were friends in college. I hadn't seen him for a long time, until we . . . me and my friend Peter here . . . came out to L.A. the other day."

"Oh, Jesus! *You're* the one!" he exclaimed with the type of laugh designed to make you feel that your pants are on backwards.

"The one what?"

"He told me yesterday he had lunch with some old friend of his."

"What's funny about that?" said Peter, his tone defensive on my behalf.

"Oh"—Lover gave a sideways glance at Peter as if not wanting to divulge anything, all the time looking as if he couldn't wait to say it—"just that Pat said your friend here tried to impress him with some cocked-up story about being in the CIA."

"What?" I sputtered, and I could feel the blood draining from my face. Peter looked at me in disbelief, and I realized that I'd forgotten to tell him that part of the story, not purposely but I'd been such an emotional wreck for other reasons when I'd returned from my lunch with Patrick.

"Yeah, we had a good laugh about it. He said you were trying to make yourself sound better than him with this bullshit story."

"That's not true," I said lamely, then added, by way of explanation, "I mean, I wasn't trying to make myself look better than him."

"Um-hm."

"Well," Peter interjected, trying to turn the conversation back to the matter at hand, "then you knew Patrick well enough to talk to him."

Lover shrugged. "You can't just spend the whole day with a dick up your ass. You've gotta talk about something."

"Then will you talk to us?"

He took his time about answering. First he took a drag from the cigarette and directed a stream of smoke at the front of my shirt. I began to feel like territory that he was marking. He reached over the railing and tapped his cigarette ash over the side. He then looked down at the ground and sighed. When he looked back up, his eyes were gleaming and the sides of his mouth had curled up into a tiny crescent-shaped smile.

"Okay. I'll be glad to talk to you."

"Great!" I said. "How about tomorrow? We'll buy you lunch."

"Oh, you don't have to do that," he replied, the little

crescent hardening. His narrowed eyes shifted from me to Peter, then back again, in a way curiously reminiscent of Jennifer Jones in *Duel in the Sun.* "You can pay me a hundred dollars for the first half hour."

"What!" I said loudly. It's a testament to the type of party this was that nobody even glanced in our direction. "We just want to talk to you!"

He shrugged. "A lot of my clients just want to talk."

The look on Peter's face told me that he almost thought this was funny. "Calm down, Alex," he said. "Mr. Lover is just a businessman."

"That's right," said Lover with a nod.

Peter looked him right in the eye and said, "You'll get it. Can you meet us at, say, ten o'clock at Santa Monica Pier?"

"You got it."

Lover started to walk away from us, then stopped, turned around, and said very pointedly, "By the way, that's one hundred, cash only."

Peter nodded and smiled.

"A hundred dollars?" I said in disbelief.

"What can we do?" said Peter with a sigh. "He gets paid for his time. We want him, we have to pay."

My incredulity gave way to resignation. I shrugged and said, "Maybe we can get the government to pay for it."

We stayed for another hour or so, trying our best to mingle and see if just maybe Patrick's murder might be the topic of conversation amongst some of the guests, so we could talk about him without intruding the subject into the discussion ourselves. Most of the talk that flitted our way consisted of "fuck this" and "fuck that" and "fucking something else," so it was hard to tell whether people were actually having a conversation or just rehearsing the lines for their next videos. Basically it was like riding the bus in Chicago. Somewhere during our canvass of the crowd, Holmes disappeared from his throne/lounge chair.

We made our way through the crowd as "YMCA" blared out from the speakers. We reached the side of the house and turned the corner to find the narrow deck deserted except for a solitary figure. There were no lights there, so he was backlit dimly by the glow from the kitchen, filtered through the living room onto which this part of the deck opened. However, we could see enough to determine that it was Derrick Holmes. When we rounded the corner he was leaning on the railing, looking out at the ocean and smoking another cigar. He looked as if he were waiting for someone. When he heard us, he turned in our direction. He had rid himself of his trunks and donned a white nylon robe that you could have seen through with cataracts, had he bothered to tie the sash that hung loosely at his sides. As it was, the robe only served to display his cock like a badge of honor. His presentation gave me the creeps. It was as if he knew what turned men on, and was contemptuous of them at the same time.

"I haven't seen you guys before," he said huskily. His voice was a cross between Lauren Bacall and Peter Lorre.

"No," I said.

"I don't know you."

"No. We were invited, though." For some reason I didn't want to say who'd invited us.

"Oh, I'm sure, I'm sure. Don't worry. I didn't mean anything. Just stating a fact."

"I'm Alex, and this is Peter."

"I see."

He leaned an elbow on the railing and looked out at the ocean again, and I felt like we were waiting for something important to happen, like lowly subjects waiting on the pleasure of the king. Despite the clamor from the patio, the air seemed to tingle with the silence that hung between the three of us.

At last he spoke. With the darkness, the scruffy beard and hair, his voice seemed to emanate eerily from the middle of nowhere. "So . . . you want to be in the movies?"

I thought for a minute about whether or not I should say I did, for the sake of our investigation. "I . . . I don't know. I think so, but I don't know."

"You have doubts."

"Uh-huh."

A short laugh floated from him. "I know just what you're thinking."

"You do?" I said, trying to sound young and credulous. It'd been a long time, but I thought I remembered what it was like.

"You're worried. I've seen it a thousand times. But there's nothing to worry about. You're worried about a lot of shit that don't matter, a lot of shit that seems important but really isn't, and if you just go ahead and do it, you'll realize that afterward. And you can make some fast money."

My stomach turned as I realized what a convincing argument that might be for a teenager or maybe somebody in their early twenties: that what you do doesn't matter; that the repercussions you fear are all smoke. It's probably really enticing to have your fears swept away so easily and have money dangled in front of you at the same time. It made me sick to think how often it probably worked. But

I pushed down what I was feeling and said what I thought should come next.

"Good money?"

There was another little laugh, and his head turned ever so slightly in our direction.

"Yeah," he said smoothly, "good money."

I hesitated again, trying to sound as if I were considering it, then said, "I'll have to think about it."

"What about you?" he said in that odd, gravelly voice. Since he didn't move, we were left to assume that he was addressing Peter.

"I think I want to." Peter let barely a beat go by before he added, "But I have to think about it, too, you know."

There was another silence, then turning away from us and back to the ocean, Holmes said, "Do that. Let me know. I'm here."

He sucked at his cigar, and we took that as our cue to leave.

"Oh great," Peter grumbled as we exited the house, "we left Chicago as nobodies, but we'll be going back as stars!"

SEVEN

As I steered the car down the incline and back onto Pacific Coast Highway, Peter said, "Alex, you know I love you and I don't think it's my place to scold you, but how could you do something as . . . as . . ."

"Stupid?"

"I was going to say 'injudicious,' but 'stupid' will do. . . . so stupid as telling Patrick Gleason that you worked for the CIA? You know we're not supposed to tell anybody."

"I know, I know! I could've kicked myself the minute it came out of my mouth!"

"Then why?"

I let out a sort of choking sigh, and glanced in the rearview mirror while I collected my thoughts. Not too far behind us was a car whose idiot driver had his brights on. I turned my attention back to the road in front of us and said, "There I was, having lunch with Patrick. . . . My old college chum had turned into—well, he was having sex for a living and excuse my bourgeois upbringing but we used to call that prostitution. . . . And even with that, and all I knew about him, he was still able to make me feel small. Even after all these years, just a few words from that sex hound and I felt ashamed of myself for being a freelance graphic artist. God, Peter, the words were out of my mouth before I knew what I was saying."

There was a silence during which I watched the road and Peter watched the side of my face. I could feel his sympathy, but it didn't make me feel much better about having been so indiscreet.

I broke the silence by saying, "Patrick always did know where to stick the knife. Like telling that Brett Lover guy about it. That was just like him. And the worst part about it is, he was right. I *was* just trying to make myself sound important."

At last Peter said softly, "I'm sorry. I guess it just boils down to being human. Don't worry about it."

"I'm not worried, really. Patrick made it clear to me that he didn't believe me. And Lover verified it."

The car behind us had inched closer and the brights were now glaring in the rearview mirror, hurting my eyes.

"Goddammit!"

Peter glanced back over his shoulder. He grimaced and said, "I thought it was getting awfully light in here."

"I wish that idiot would either dim his goddamn brights or pass us."

As if the driver of the car had heard me, he pulled to the left and sped up, the lights boring into the side mirror, reflecting off it like a searchlight and almost blinding me.

"Jesus!"

The car swerved back into the lane behind us, and continued to gain on us until it was just one car length away. I tried not to speed up, thinking that the only thing that could make matters worse would be to find ourselves in a high-speed chase on a road I didn't know well, but I found that my body parts had developed a life of their own. Even though I kept telling myself not to speed up, my foot inched the gas pedal closer to the floor, and we were going faster and faster. At the same time, I tried as hard as I could to see who was driving the car, but the brights flashed off the rearview mirrors and made identification of the driver or the license plates impossible. Hell, the damn lights were so intense I couldn't even tell what kind of car it was.

"Get in the right lane," said Peter anxiously. "Let him pass!"

"I don't think he wants to pass!" I said loudly, but I thought his idea was as good as any. I fought my good-driver impulse to put on the turn signal, and instead I swung quickly into the right lane.

"Jeez!" said Peter, shielding his eyes.

Our pursuer hit the gas as if his intention had always been simply to pass us, but when the car had finally reached a point where if it went forward any further its headlights would be partially blocked by the side of our car and we might be able to get a glimpse of the driver, he stopped his advance. I was just about to heave a hesitant sigh of relief when there was a loud bang and my steering wheel jerked violently to the left. I fought to turn it back, but we found ourselves crossing the two opposite lanes— directly into oncoming traffic.

I realized right away that our tire had blown. At first I thought we'd hit the car that'd been following us, but he'd immediately fallen back and I lost sight of him. Two oncoming cars split to the left and right as we dove between them. It took all my adrenaline-enhanced strength to turn the steering wheel far enough to send our car headed back to the right side of the road, but the effort was too much for me, and the moment we were on the right, the wheel swirled counterclockwise like a loosened spring, and we swerved over to the far left of the other side. By the grace of God, we just missed a northbound car as Peter joined me in trying to regain control of the steering wheel, but we were already way too far out of control. The car fishtailed as we ran up the ridge as far as we could before the front of the car jammed into the dirt. In one of those startling, movielike moments I saw the hood of the car waffle, and realized that the back of the car was still moving. The impact and angle at which we'd hit this hill had stopped the front of the car in its tracks, but the back of the car slid sideways up the ridge, and we hung there for a moment like a motorized lizard clinging to the side of a wall. But it was only for a moment.

"Grab something!" I yelled.

We had not gone far up the embankment, but far enough for the car to roll over on its way back down to the road. I learned at that moment that actually being in a car that's rolling over is *nothing* like it is in the movies. It's messy. The two of us were dropped onto the ceiling and then clung for dear life to the inner side of the bucket seats and the steering wheel to not come in contact with the ground as the passenger window rolled over the dirt. Peter groaned with pain as the hand with which he held on to the steering wheel was wrenched around, and both of us found our grips slipping as the car rolled. As it started to right itself we were both dumped onto the floor. The car bounced on its tires against the road and tilted sideways toward the passenger side, but it had lost its momentum and recoiled back to the road on the driver's side, a loud metallic thud running through us as the hub of the flat tire hit the pavement.

The sudden silence and lack of movement came as if we'd suddenly gone deaf. I pulled myself up from the floor and onto the seat, hitting my head on the steering wheel in the process. Peter looked as if he'd been stuffed under the glove compartment. He groaned, and I said frantically, "Are you all right?"

He turned his face up toward me. There was a small cut just beneath his hairline. "You've got to be kidding."

I was really as close to hysteria as I've ever been. "Peter! Are you all right?" I shouted.

He let out a little groan and started to shift himself off of the floor, grabbing the side of his seat to pull himself up.

"Yes I'm all right, considering that I've just survived a practical demonstration of how to mix cement."

I sighed and could feel my insides shake, as if now that we'd survived, the relief was going to blow me apart. I knew if he was talking that way, no serious damage had been done.

"Well," I said, trying to recover from the shock, "*there's* an argument for wearing seat belts."

"Alex," said Peter suddenly, "will this thing run?"

"I don't know," I said, barely paying attention.

"Alex, get us the hell off this highway!"

I looked up and saw what Peter had seen: we had ended up in the middle of the northbound lanes beside the ridge—only, we were facing south. And there was traffic coming. I turned the keys in the ignition, and the engine sputtered for a moment, then stopped. I tried again with the same results. We could see the headlights getting closer. I know most people would find their lives flashing before their eyes at this point, but all my brain was doing was replaying the end of *Poltergeist*. I gave the ignition one more sharp turn, and the engine caught, though it didn't sound happy about it. I grabbed the shift and pushed it into Drive. The car limped rather than lurched across the road, and came to rest with a reluctant sputter on the shoulder of the other side.

"That was really fun," said Peter wryly. "What do you plan for us for tomorrow?"

EIGHT

Mother was quite displeased when she arrived for breakfast the next morning and found us still in bed. She was even more displeased about our condition. Peter and I were bruised pretty badly, but fortunately had not required a lot of bandaging. There were a couple of miraculously minor scrapes on Peter's right arm, and there was a gash on my knee where I'd hit the brake pedal when I slipped off the seat and onto the floor as we'd tumbled. But the real reason for our exhaustion was that we'd spent several hours afterward explaining to the police and the rental car company that the car had gone out of control when we had a blowout. That was the simple explanation, and it got us out of there more quickly than we would have if we'd reported to them what we really thought: that someone had shot the tire out. And what could we have told them? Only that it was done by someone in a car we couldn't identify, and we hadn't even seen the direction in which our pursuer had gone. The ramifications would have had us with the police for the remainder of the night. And simplifying the explanation had also gotten the rental company to replace the car with a lot less trouble. As one could expect, they were not exactly pleased with the condition of the car, which would never work for them again, but the blowout explanation had some rather serious negligence implications that the company was eager to quash before they even got started. We were supplied a teal-blue Chevy Lumina that had more miles on it than any rental I've ever used. I got the feeling that the company was a little reluctant to allow someone who'd totaled one of their cars have a brand-new one, no matter what the reason for the accident.

"This is getting too dangerous for us, luvey," said Mother as we had croissants on the balcony. Even in our bruised, battered, and generally nerve-racked condition, we weren't about to set aside the niceties. "We should let the police handle it."

"There's two things wrong with that," I said, washing some of the flaky pastry down with iced tea. "One is that the police *aren't* handling the murder, as far as I know. They gave me every impression that they were going to blow it off."

"And the second?"

"We set up a meeting with Brett Lover for ten o'clock this morning. We have no way of canceling so instead of standing him up, which is definitely contrary to the way you raised me—"

"I really do hate it when you throw that up at me."

". . . so instead of standing him up, we might as well keep the appointment and see what we can see. And there's

102

one other thing: I think the events of last night prove we're on to something."

Mother sighed and turned to Peter, as if under the circumstances she wasn't above trying to divide and conquer. "Do you agree with him?"

"I really don't like it when somebody tries to kill me," Peter said. He raised a steaming cup of coffee to his mouth.

"I would find that a lot funnier, darling, if I weren't so worried."

"Did you make any progress at the apartment building?"

"Oh yes," Mother replied with a sly smile. "I spent my time yesterday, at least while there was still light, doing window boxes."

Both Peter and I stopped in the act of stuffing our respective faces.

"What?" we said in unison.

"Window boxes. I always think that a house isn't a home without window boxes."

"You were supposed to be trying to find things out!"

She gave me a mock-disparaging glance and said, "Oh, how little faith you have in me! I was working on window boxes on the walkway. I was out there all afternoon, so I got to speak to all of my neighbors."

Peter smiled. "Jean, only you would have thought of gardening as detection."

"And just as I thought, the murder was the talk of the building. Everyone was all a-buzz about it. There's a young woman lives next door to me who said she's moving out the minute her lease is up. She doesn't think she'll get another moment's sleep as long as she lives there, poor dear. There's an older gentleman lives below me, and we had quite a long conversation about safety and such over the railing—I mean, I was leaning over the railing talking to him while he looked up at me from the garden."

"Like the balcony scene in *Romeo and Juliet*," I said with sonlike snideness.

"Don't be daft, darling," she replied, then took another sip of her tea. "Anyway, I didn't get anything in the way of useful information from them, because they said they never really got to know Patrick, and what little they knew they didn't like. They seemed to think he was a prig."

"What?" said Peter, choking on his coffee.

"A *prig*, dear. Whatever did you think I said?"

"Nothing," Peter replied with an embarrassed smile as he wiped the coffee from his chin.

"So you didn't find out anything?" I asked.

"Oh, don't be too sure about that," Mother said slyly. "There's more than two other residents, you know. But I'll admit, I didn't get much of anything until Mr. Watkins came home from work."

"Mr. Watkins?"

"Reg Watkins. He's a very nice young gentleman who lives two doors down from me. He dresses very well, and he's very polite."

"So was Crippen, by all accounts."

"What did he tell you?" Peter asked.

"That I wasn't arranging the flowers properly. He gave me the name of a good greenhouse where I might get flats of petunias. He said he always thought petunias looked nice in window boxes."

I heaved an exaggerated sigh. There are times when I'm really not sure whether or not Mother's pulling my leg. I said, "About *Patrick*, Mother!"

She looked confused for a moment, then said, "Oh, yes!

He was quite disturbed about the murder, as was everyone else in the building, but he had a different reason."

This piqued our interest. "What was it?"

"Mr. Watkins is gay, dear, and he's sure that the murder was a gay thing—that that was why Patrick was murdered."

Peter clucked his tongue and sat back in his chair, "Oh, great. There's something we hadn't thought of: gay paranoia."

"Wait a minute," I said, "how did he know Pat was gay? Did he have something to do with him?"

Mother smiled knowingly, "That's exactly what I asked him—I mean, how he knew. As it turns out, Mr. Watkins didn't know Patrick personally, though I gather it wasn't for want of trying. No, he knew about Patrick's work."

"I see."

"No no no, I don't mean that he's seen Patrick's videos, I mean he was assuming about what Patrick did for a living."

"Why on earth would he assume that Patrick had something to do with porn?" asked Peter.

"Because of one of his visitors," Mother replied triumphantly.

Her face told us that she'd gotten the reaction she'd hoped for: Peter and I both raised our eyebrows, and Peter added a "Hmmm."

"Who was his visitor? Someone Watkins recognized?"

"Yes . . . someone named Syd Wishes, which I assume is a stage name. I can't imagine anyone really having that for a name."

"Oh yeah, Syd Wishes," I said. Mother and Peter each turned to me, with different degrees of surprise.

I shrugged. Once having made the slip, there was no

use denying it. "I've seen him before. . . . I mean his videos." I turned to Peter and added, "Before I met you."

Peter said, "Pretty soon I'll be looking for a job where I don't have to work any evenings. You need a nanny."

"*Before* I met you," I emphasized.

"Never mind."

I turned to Mother, hoping to change the subject quickly, and said, "So this Watkins recognized Syd Wishes?"

"Oh yes, he was quite sure about it."

"And Watkins told you all this while you were out there potting plants? God, Mother, I've underestimated your abilities."

"Yes, he did, poor thing. I get the impression that Mr. Watkins is lonely. He hasn't had any visitors since I've been here."

"That hasn't been that long."

"I know, but he sounded just like a lost puppy when he told me Patrick hadn't been very friendly. It's very sad, that. Maybe the two of you could try to fix him up with someone while we're out here."

"Mother, the only person we know out here is dead."

She shrugged and said, "Well, yes, there's that."

"Well," said Peter, "you really *have* been keeping your eyes open, haven't you."

She shrugged. "It's what I was told to do."

"That's another thing that's bothering me," I said. "Good old Agent Larry Nelson, our man in Washington. Why the hell did he tell you to do that?"

"I don't know. But I did put a call in to him yesterday, to tell him about the murder, in which he was supremely uninterested—or at least, that's the way he seemed. With him it's hard to tell. And I also asked him to find out what he could about Mano Man Productions."

"What did he say?"

"Nothing yet. He said he'd see if they had anything—but . . ."

"Yes?" I prodded her impatiently.

"Nothing," she said, shaking her head. "It's just that he sounded so damned evasive about the whole thing."

"That's how Nelson sounds about everything," I said.

Mother thought for a moment, making a smacking sound with her lips. "At any rate, I'm sure they'll come up with something."

"They probably will," said Peter sardonically. "I'll bet they keep quite a file on all things gay. Especially successful gay enterprises."

"Do you really think they're that successful?" said Mother.

I answered her. "I'm sure there's a hell of a lot of money in it. Look at how many video stores there are in the country, all with gay customers who're always looking for some new fun."

"Not *all* of them," Peter said with a sly smile. The implication wasn't lost on me. I blushed.

"So what do we do now?" said Mother.

I glanced at the clock on the nightstand and said, "Well, right now I think we'd better go and see what Brett Lover can tell us. Last night I got the feeling that he knew more about Patrick than he was willing to tell us."

"For free, you mean," said Peter as we rose from the table.

"Oh, that reminds me, Mother—do you have a hundred dollars?"

There was a fair amount of bustle along the extensive length of Santa Monica Pier, although this early in the day the famed merry-go-round lay dormant in its roundhouse. I peered in the windows, and the darkness inside made the motionless horses loom ominously in their circle, as if a sudden burst of power might send them rampaging through the countryside.

The three of us walked almost to the end of the pier, along which men of assorted races stood fishing. Just before the arch (or pavilion or whatever they call it) were a bunch of benches facing various directions. Peter sat beside me on one facing east, toward the entrance to the pier. This would give us a good enough view to see Lover approaching, and since directly behind the bench was a railing and a straight drop into the ocean, we could be fairly certain that nobody would be able to cross behind us and listen unnoticed, though at this point we had no way of knowing why anyone would want to do that. Mother took a seat on a bench catty-corner to ours, facing north.

The sky was hazy with smog and the sun was trying to eat its way through, which put the light at that irritating level where it's too bright for the naked eye and too dark for sunglasses. There was quite a bit of activity around the various ramshackle shops, some just opening and some in full swing, apparently catering to tourists who had not yet adjusted to Pacific Standard Time (since there didn't appear to be anything about the shops that would interest the fishermen, whom I took to be the only locals who would be out there at ten in the morning). There were more than enough customers along the pier to make being open at that hour worth the shopkeepers' while.

In fact, the number of people strolling around made me feel both safer and more apprehensive. Safe because there's safety in numbers; apprehensive because it was extremely difficult to keep track of who was around. As Mother had pointed out earlier, whatever we'd happened into out here had become quite a bit more dangerous, and I would've felt a lot better about this meeting if I could be sure it was unobserved.

I glanced at the watch that I normally wear on trips. "He's late."

"How late?" said Peter.

"Seven minutes so far."

"Humph," Peter snorted. "That's hardly late. I'm sure people like Brett Lover have a different way of telling time—like ten o'clock means whenever the hell he happens to get out of bed and haul himself here. If he shows up at all."

"You have to be patient, the both of you," Mother interjected, "he'll probably be here. Seven minutes isn't even fashionably late."

We sat quietly for a couple of minutes; then I said, "You know, I just thought of something. It's just possible that Lover had something to do with that 'accident' of ours last night."

"How do you figure that?"

"Well, think of it. Remember, we didn't want to go around asking people if they'd known Patrick, because we didn't want to draw attention to ourselves. Lover was the only one we talked to directly about it."

"So?"

"So . . . if he thought we were looking into Patrick's murder, and he had something to do with it, he might have tried to get rid of us."

"I don't know, sweetheart," said Peter, shaking his head. "I didn't get the impression that Lover could see past his own reflection."

I pressed on, warming to the idea and disliking its implications at the same time. "But if he *did* have something to do with it, then that means—"

"That means it's not exactly bright for us to be meeting him like this," said Mother, her voice taking on the slight Cockney accent she tends toward when she wants to make a point.

"No," said Peter, laying a calming hand on her knee, "this would be exactly what we should do. If he thought we were killed last night, he won't show up, so I wouldn't worry about it."

"Whoever chased us didn't wait around to make sure we were dead. He might show up just to be certain."

"Which would still make this the place to be," Peter explained. "If he's involved, we need to talk to him. And if he wasn't involved, we still need to talk to him about Patrick, which is why we wanted to meet him in the first place. This is a very public place. Nobody would try anything here."

Both Mother and I turned away from him and sighed. There didn't seem to be any way to logically disagree with him, especially since he was right.

People continued to amble past us: a couple wearing identical shirts with broad blue and yellow stripes, as if they were afraid they'd get separated in a crowd and wanted to be easy to spot; a blond boy who looked much too young to be out there alone rode by on a small red bike; and several other people both singly and in pairs, who had that look that tourists get when they visit a place that's supposed to be famous and can't figure out what all the fuss is about.

The combination of the haze, the plaintive cries of gulls, and the meandering quality of the passersby made the whole scene seem forbidding to me. It took on a feeling of unreality, like everything had gone silent and everyone was moving in slow motion through waves of heat.

It was almost twenty after ten when I looked way down toward the entrance to the pier and thought I could just make out Brett Lover coming down the ramp along with a fresh flock of tourists. Most of the little shops had gone into full swing. People were gazing at racks of picture postcards, holding T-shirts and sweatshirts up to their chests to see if they liked the size and the design, and bells, whistles, and shouts rang out from a dark, cavernous video arcade not far from where we were sitting. There was much more activity than I was comfortable with.

By the time the man reached the bottom of the ramp I knew it was Lover. He strutted with that "I am the king of all I survey" attitude that he'd demonstrated so clearly last night.

"There he is," I said, nodding in his direction. Peter looked toward the entrance, spotted Lover, and smiled.

" 'I am the master of my soul,' " he said sardonically.

"Which one is he?" said mother.

"The popinjay," I replied.

Peter explained a little more fully. "Walking down the center of the pier—muted yellow pants, floral shirt."

"Hmmm."

Lover continued to swagger his way toward us, looking from side to side, checking out the benches for us and checking out the men who passed by—or, I should say, letting the men check him out. In the light of day, he looked less exotic but no less attractive. His tan was a lot more evident, and his hair more blond; unlike last night, it was fetchingly tousled, as if it were being done by a wind machine on an MGM soundstage. He looked preppy and innocent, which I'm sure got him a lot of work in porn.

When he was about two hundred feet away, he spotted us and a smug smile spread across his face. I really didn't like that smile. It had the look of sexual superiority of someone who always winds up on top, both in the bedroom and out of it. He looked like he fucked people for a living in more ways than one. He turned in our direction at a leisurely pace, happy to be late and happy to make us wait even a little bit longer.

When he was about twenty feet from us, he opened his mouth as if he were about to say something; then, suddenly, his head jerked forward so fast that his chin bounced against his chest and back again, and a split second later his chest thrust forward as if someone had punched him in the back. To say the least, I was startled, and my mind suddenly flashed to *Alien*, when the creature pops out of John Hurt. But there was no such obvious evidence of what had caused the obscene spasm. Lover's legs buckled and he fell to his knees; his torso swayed a moment in a sickly, circular motion, and he finally fell backward and to the side.

"Oh, my Lord," said Mother in a whisper as she stared saucer-eyed at Lover. Her words sounded quietly in the dead silence just before pandemonium broke out on the pier. The crowd scrambled wildly in all directions at once, people running into each other, slamming together and falling, and recovering and running in other directions.

I ran to Lover, with Mother and Peter right behind me. As I started to kneel beside him I noticed the blood for the first time. I looked up at Peter and said frantically, "Go! Quick, see if you can find him!"

Peter looked at me quizzically for a moment, then realized that what I meant was that we needed to see if he could find anyone on the pier that he recognized. He nodded at me and took off toward the entrance. Of course, in my panic I didn't realize that it would be a futile effort to try to find anyone in this stampeding crowd.

Gurgling noises came from Lover's throat as I cradled his head in my lap. Mother pulled his legs from beneath him in an attempt to straighten him out and make him more comfortable. I stroked his hair and noticed with a guilty pang that the smile to which I'd been mentally objecting just a few moments earlier had gone. I felt the back of his head and my stomach lurched when my fingers found a gash that I assumed to be a bullet hole: Then I ran my hand below his shoulders and found another just about in the middle of his back.

"Oh Jesus God, he's been shot," I said, stating the obvious.

Lover let out a loud humming sound, as if he were trying to shout himself awake from the middle of a nightmare and couldn't get his mouth to work, and then there was a spasm that caused his back to arch in a manner that was painful to watch. He slowly relaxed and straightened; then his head drooped sideways and a stream of blood flowed from the corner of his mouth.

"He's dead," said Mother quietly.

Then we heard the sirens.

In the course of the first CIA case into which I stumbled, I saw one man shot through the head and another fall off the top of the Sears Tower; but in both cases, it happened to someone who was in the process of trying to kill me. It was something quite different to see someone shot who was merely trying to talk to me, someone whose worst sin (as far as I knew) was attempting to extort a little money in exchange for information. It was something really different, and I'd be lying if I said I wasn't affected by it. The last thing I needed at that moment was to be grilled by the police. Unfortunately, the police are a lot less sympathetic the second time you turn up with a dead body on your hands.

So when Mother and I found ourselves back at police headquarters, Detective Rob Furness was not amused. This time we weren't offered coffee and we weren't given the "luxury" of a casual conversation with him and his partner, Detective Howard Hemple (who had taken Mother's statement the first time) in the squad room. We were taken to an interrogation room: a bleak little place with a hardwood table and half a dozen hard, straight-backed chairs. Peter escaped this because he hadn't returned to the scene by the time the police took us away.

Furness looked at Mother and said, "So, Miss . . . Robbins, was it? Are you going to offer an alibi for Reynolds here? You seem to pop up pretty conveniently by his side."

Mother stared at him for a moment, deciding how to proceed. But before she could, Furness continued:

"I know—you just happened to be strolling on the pier this morning, and just happened to see this guy get shot, and you just happen to be able to swear that Reynolds here didn't have nothing to do with it."

Mother sighed, getting impatient with the monologue. "Mr. Furness, as it happens . . ."

"As it happens . . ." said Furness, mimicking her. I didn't want to give him the satisfaction of making me angry, but I could see it was going to be hard. He continued, "You should probably proceed with caution. I don't know what kinda game the two of you are playing, but this is where it ends. You're sure not going to tell me it was a coincidence that you were there at the same time. Were you about to give me another cock-and-bull story about how you don't know Reynolds here?"

"As it happens," said Mother with pointed primness, "Alex is my son."

"Your son," said Furness flatly. He sounded as if he'd been prepared to feign shock no matter what my mother said. Unfortunately for him, he actually did look surprised.

"Yes, he's my son."

"So, is your name Robbins?" Furness said to me.

Mother got that look that I imagine anyone would have who suddenly felt that every untruth they'd ever told was about to come out.

"No," she said apologetically, "my name is Jean Reynolds."

"So what were you doing living in the same building as one of the victims, under an assumed name, no less?"

Mother looked down at the floor, and I could feel for her. It was hard enough to explain it to me, I can't imagine how she'd explain it to the police. She could possibly offer a reasonable explanation for why she'd come out to L.A. to see Patrick, but it would be much more difficult to explain how she'd managed to be in the same apartment building without bringing Agent Nelson into the picture. And under the present circumstances, I doubted the police would believe her if she explained that she was using an assumed name as a lark.

"It's a little difficult . . . it's a personal matter."

"You think so, huh?" said Furness with disgust. "Well, we'll see about that. And we'll get back to you in a minute."

"But, Detective Furness, everything else I told you when we were here before was true."

"Was it?"

"Alex was not at Patrick Gleason's apartment before he was killed. He really did arrive and discover the body, and he really wasn't in the apartment long enough to have done it himself."

"And this Brett Lover guy?"

"We told you what happened. We told you that he was killed in front of us, and that we didn't see who did it. There must've been a hundred other people there who could tell you the same thing."

"Unfortunately, nobody was paying enough attention. The only people we got hold of said that all they saw was that Lover got shot as he was approaching *your son*." I got the impression he was emphasizing the words not so much to implicate me in the murder as to remind my mother that because of her previous lies, he didn't exactly feel the need to trust her.

"I can tell you that Alex didn't have anything to do with this young man's shooting. But—"

"And there we have another one of those coincidences. This 'young man' just happened to be another porn star." Furness turned his deceptively lazy-looking green eyes on me and said, "Tell me something, Reynolds. You ever heard of Jack the Ripper?"

"What?" I said.

"Jack the Ripper. You've heard of him, haven't you?"

"Yes," I said quietly. I had an awful feeling about which way this was going to go.

"So what have you got against these porn guys? You think they give you people a bad name?"

"If by 'you people' you mean gays, then no. I don't think that gays who appear in porn give gays a bad name . . . any more than breeders who appear in porn give breeders a bad name."

I chose that particular pejorative for straight people to get back at him, and because it was the only one I could think of. That's the trouble with living in a predominantly straight world: the majority tends to keep itself from being labeled. But the word did have an effect on Furness. He looked affronted and surprised, as if the idea that there might be derogatory terms for straight people had never even occurred to him. But I doubted it had the same effect as calling someone a faggot.

Furness decided to try again. "So what do you have against these guys that fuck for money?"

"I don't have anything against them."

"You a religious man?"

"No," I said with more contempt than I'd intended. I had nothing against religion, just religion in the way I took him to mean it at that moment. It was proof that you could turn any word into a pejorative.

"You sure? You know, those guys in those videos, they're sinning against God, aren't they?"

"I would think that if they're hurting anyone, they're only hurting themselves."

Mother cut in, "That's why I came out here, and why Alex got in touch with Patrick in the first place. Alex was surprised to find out that Patrick was doing those types of videos, so he wanted to try and talk to him about it."

I'm sure Mother thought she was helping me when she said that, but Furness's face beamed with triumph.

"So you *do* think there's something wrong with those porn guys, huh?"

"Oh come on, Detective! I don't think it's a healthy lifestyle, and neither do you. You said as much earlier. You can't make anything out of that."

"Tell me something," said Furness, leaning in toward me with a smarmy smile spread across his face. "How did you learn that your old friend was making dirty movies?"

You know, it was at that moment I realized that renting that goddamn tape was a social faux pas from which I would never recover.

"I saw him," I said.

"So you watch porn, do you?" His smile was even more triumphant.

"Lots of people do things they're not proud of. You can't make anything of that, either."

Furness's look of triumph turned to barely controlled anger. "I'll tell you what I can make something out of: the fact that I've found you with two dead faggots—and the 'alibi' you have for the murder of Patrick Gleason is your mother, who is living in the building under an assumed name."

You know, when he put it that way, I really did look like the son of Ma Barker.

Mother tried again, and the minute she opened her mouth, I really wished that she would close it, because I had a feeling that anything she said was going to make things worse.

"Detective, you *know* that Alex didn't have anything to do with Patrick's murder. You're experienced enough to know that Patrick had been dead a long time before we called you."

Furness just shrugged. "So you were smart—so you waited a while after you killed him before you called us."

"You don't believe that!"

Furness barreled in on her. "So why did *you* come out here, Mrs. Reynolds? Did your son go berserk when he saw his friend in the video? He start talking about killing him? Maybe you came out here because you wanted to stop him?"

"Oh, don't be idiotic!" Mother said dismissively.

Furness smirked at her quaintness in a way that made me long to use a cudgel on him. "Well how 'bout this: maybe you wanted to warn Gleason and he didn't believe you."

"I came out here for the reason I stated, nothing more."

I'm sure she wondered, as I did, whether or not Furness was going to pursue the matter of her lodgings. But before he could, there was a knock at the door. Hemple opened it. Someone whispered something to him, and he in turn whispered something to Furness. Furness looked irritated, said, "I'll be right back," and left the room.

He was gone several minutes, during which Hemple sat quietly by the door. Neither Mother nor I were dumb enough to discuss what was going on with Hemple in the room. As a matter of fact, we wouldn't have discussed things even if he wasn't in the room: I'd seen enough movies with bugged interrogation rooms or two-way glass. The one thing Mother did do was ask how I was.

"I'm all right," I replied, feeling really tired now that I had a moment to think about it. "I'm all right." Then I looked at Hemple, who was giving every indication of not listening though we knew he couldn't help but hear us. I added loudly, "But it's not easy to see somebody shot. And now we have to sit here like idiots answering these stupid questions."

"Now, Alex . . ." said Mother, who then glanced at Hemple and stopped whatever she was going to say. I had the feeling that she'd been about to remark upon the fact that the police couldn't help but grill us, given the compromising positions in which we'd found ourselves during the past couple of days. At least, that's what I was thinking myself.

After an endless wait, during which Hemple tried very hard not to show that he was getting impatient, Furness walked briskly back into the room looking cowed and irritated. He stood at the head of the table and looked both of us in the eye in turn. "You're free to go."

Mother and I, and even Hemple, said "What?" at the same time.

"You heard me: you're free to go. There's someone waiting outside for you."

"Who?"

"Go on," he said, waving his hand testily in the direction of the door.

Mother and I glanced at each other, then rose slowly from the table, almost as if we were expecting a trick of some kind. When we reached the door, Furness shot his arm across it and blocked our way. He narrowed his eyes and said, "But I'll tell you something, you better not even think of leaving this town without telling me, you got that?" He looked at me as if he were sure that I thought I was getting away with something. A knowing smile spread over his face and his eyes got even more narrow. "I'm not a fool, Reynolds. Even Jack the Ripper had friends in high places."

He dropped his arm and stepped out of the way. We walked past him and out into the squad room. Standing in the middle of the room, in his Mormonesque blue suit, looking as if he thought his overly dignified demeanor might be permanently soiled by bringing it to a lowly police station, was Agent Lawrence Nelson.

NINE

To say I was surprised to see him would seriously un-
derstate the case. I knew his presence signified that something was seriously wrong. Nelson never "just happened to
be in the neighborhood," and I couldn't believe that he'd
flown all the way from D.C. to L.A. for the express purpose
of rescuing us from the hands of the police, let alone the
fact that there hadn't been enough time: it'd been less than
two hours since Brett Lover was shot. And Nelson's love for
us wouldn't take him from Washington to Arlington, not
to mention Los Angeles. He'd never shown any great fond-
ness for us. Then again, he rarely showed any emotion at
all.

The feelings were decidedly mutual: I refer to him by
surname only (something that I'm usually too polite to do)
because, although he's my "boss" on the occasions that we
work for the government, I don't like him. But then, how
many people like their bosses?

Nelson wordlessly led us from Nazi headquarters (as I'd affectionately come to think of it) to his car. Once outside, I asked him how he'd known where we were.

"I called your hotel when I arrived in town. Your . . . roommate told me what had happened."

"My husband," I said flatly, irritated with his insistence on calling Peter my roommate, even though he knew better.

"Whatever."

Nelson climbed into the car and Mother got in front beside him. I took the back, which would have made conversation a little disconcerting had he chosen to talk at all. But he informed us at the outset that he wanted to wait to talk until he had the three of us together, so he started the car and headed for our hotel. I was left to contemplate the back of his perfectly shaped head. I would rather have looked inside of it.

I once described Nelson as swarthy, and I'll stick by that description. He has dark hair, dark skin, and eyes so dark brown they are almost black. It irritates me that he's so handsome. Every time I've seen him he's been wearing the requisite government-issue navy blue suit and exhibiting the demeanor to go with it. You'd have thought he had a pole up his ass, if he were able to get it open far enough to admit one.

"My, my my . . . this is nice," said Nelson, looking around as he walked into our hotel room. "Nothing like my room at the Beaumont. The government isn't paying for this."

"The government hasn't been asked to," said Peter sharply. Then he turned to me and said, "God, I'm sorry I lost you. I couldn't find anybody I recognized. By the time I got back you were gone."

I shook my head with resignation. "It was a madhouse. Whoever shot Lover was probably halfway off the pier before we even knew what had happened."

"Lor', I need some tea," said Mother. "I feel I've been through the wringer."

"I'll call room service," said Peter.

I noticed for the first time since the shooting that Mother really did look a little pale. It then occurred to me that though she'd been an integral part of our government doings, this was the first time she'd been present when someone was killed. For me it was getting to be old hat.

"Are you all right?" I asked.

"Oh yes," she said, waving me off as she dropped into the chair by the little circular table. "I just thought we were going to end up in the 'oosgow before Larry showed up. We were all for it up till then."

Now I knew she was upset. Whenever she started dropping her aitches it was a sure sign that she was more distressed than she'd let on.

Peter was just hanging up the phone when I asked Nelson, "What exactly *did* bring you to our aid?"

"I wasn't coming to your aid," he said perfunctorily as he dropped his briefcase on the bed. "I didn't even know you'd been experiencing difficulties until I arrived."

That was the essential difference between Agent Lawrence Nelson and most of the rest of the human race. He saw our present situation as a difficulty; I saw it as a crisis.

"You knew that my friend had been killed—Mother told you that much on the phone."

"Well, yes," he said with a little shrug, "but while the death of anyone *may* be regrettable . . ."

My dander flew up at the way he emphasized the word "may."

". . . it's not usually of any particular consequence. I mean to the general workings of the government."

"Then why did you come out here?" Peter asked.

Nelson exuded professional distance as if he were emanating armor. He was like a human extension of the Martian ships in *The War of the Worlds*.

"I came here to tell you that it's time for you to go back to Chicago."

That is probably the only thing he could have said that would have gotten Mother back to her feet. She rose slowly, her eyes riveted on Nelson. He hadn't exactly lost the interest of Peter and me, either. I couldn't believe what I'd just heard.

"What?" said Mother.

"I'm sure you understood what I just said."

"I understood the words, yes," said Mother, "but I can't think what you mean by them."

"I meant exactly what I said. It's time for you to return to Chicago."

This is one of the aspects of Nelson's personality that I've never been able to get used to: his propensity for delivering information like this as if it required no further explanation. He metes out details like individual seeds of grain to the starving Third World masses, and it's always been obvious that he considers *us* to be very low on the food chain.

"Why?" I said. "Do you have a job for us?"

"No."

"Then why on earth should we leave here?" Mother was beginning to sound absolutely indignant.

126

"Wait a minute," said Peter, "you came all the way out here to tell us that? Couldn't you just use the phone?"

"No," he said simply. "It was important that I come here."

"Well, as much as I appreciate your smoothing over our trouble with the police, I must say you have a hell of a nerve," Mother said hotly. "You expect us to go home simply because you come in here and say we should, with no reason whatsoever? I'm afraid we'll have to disappoint you on that. We can't leave now, we have a lot to do."

"I want you to leave this alone."

"My friend has been killed!" I said.

"I'm sure the police will take care of that."

"No, they won't. Their view of Patrick is no better than—" I had started to say "no better than yours," but there's confrontation and there's confrontation. I wasn't prepared to cross the line with Nelson, at least until we knew why he was really here. I settled for a more minor attack.

"I can't explain it to somebody like you, but I have every reason to believe that they'll just write it off."

"A good policeman will only write off a murder if he's sure he can't solve it. Whether or not they accomplish that has nothing more to do with you. Though you've been of some little assistance to my department . . ."

Peter emitted a "Hmph" at that one.

Nelson shot him a glance and continued, ". . . you *can't* believe that you would be any more capable of solving a murder than the professionals."

Peter started to say something, but Mother laid a hand on his arm to stop him.

"So far," she said, "I haven't heard anything that you

127

couldn't have told us over the phone. Surely you didn't expect us to react any differently in person."

He sighed again in that way he had of trying to make the three of us feel as if we were being tiresome children.

"I suppose I didn't."

"There's more going on here than just the murder of two young men, isn't there?" I said.

There was a long pause during which Nelson looked at the floor. He seemed to be debating with himself. He finally raised his head and said, "Your being here may have seriously jeopardized an ongoing investigation."

"An investigation? Since when does the CIA look into domestic matters?" said mother.

Peter added, "I thought your local duties were cut back due to Watergate."

Nelson ignored Peter and responded to Mother, sounding exactly as if he were a tour guide at the U.N. "Our precise activities may seem a bit murky to the public in general. Our activities encompass many different things and may, on occasion, require our involvement in domestic issues."

"Oh, my God," I said, sinking onto the bed and putting my face in my hands. "It was Mother's call, wasn't it? When she asked you about Mano Man Productions."

Nelson didn't even bother looking at me. He simply continued to face Mother as if I wasn't speaking.

"That's what brought you out here. It's organized crime, isn't it? You're investigating organized crime and the porn industry."

Nelson turned to me without changing expression. "My department would not be conducting such an investigation."

"Then why are we even having this conversation?" said Peter angrily. Peter has far less use for Nelson than I do.

"Surely you didn't come out here just to spring us from jail," said Mother. Forties-movie lingo sounded a lot funnier with an English accent. "And surely you didn't come all the way out here just to warn us off. What's going on, Larry?"

"That's *exactly* what I came here to do," said Nelson, sounding ruffled for the first time. "Warn you off. You've blundered into something important, and we need for you to get out of it."

"What? What have we blundered into?" I said.

He glanced down at his briefcase as if there were something in it he would sorely like to use on us: like a blackjack, or a gun. A muscle twitched on his right jaw, and I realized that this was the first time I'd ever seen him struggle with himself. It was clear to me that he was aggravated at our insistence on more details, and at the same time understood that he couldn't expect us to pack up and leave just because he said to. I'll bet he wished it could be that easy.

"Jean, you know we only discuss facts that are pertinent to cases on which you're working, and at that we only tell you facts that are absolutely essential to your participation."

"Would you please stop talking like a training manual," said Mother.

He went on unperturbed. "What is going on here is something in which you are *not* involved, and as such you know I can't tell you anything about it. The only thing I *can* tell you is that now your continued presence here may cause more trouble."

I have to admit that at that point, if he'd said "please," I might have been inclined to consider leaving. I wouldn't have gone, but I would have felt a lot guiltier about staying. However, I don't think Nelson would say "please" if you bit his balls.

Before Mother could reply, I drew myself up and said, "Sorry, Nelson, it's not enough. Patrick was a friend of mine, and we intend to find out who killed him."

"Yeah," said Peter, seconding me, "and if Patrick's death wasn't enough, then seeing Brett Lover killed right in front of us this morning tore it. We're staying."

Mother was silent, but she raised her eyebrows in a way that was as much as to say, "So there!"

"You know," Nelson said at last, "I could have just left you at the jail."

"Then why didn't you?" I said.

The look on his face told me that he realized his outburst (albeit a quiet one) had been an indiscretion. And after watching him for a moment, a more drastic realization hit me.

"You didn't *want* us in there, did you? You didn't want us to talk to them!"

Nelson paused dramatically for a moment before reaching down for his briefcase and saying, "Very well. I've said what I came to say." He checked the latch of the briefcase as if he suspected it might have been tampered with while we talked. I tried not to take offense. "But the help I gave you this afternoon is the last I can offer. If you're going to stay here against the wishes of the government, then I won't be able to bail you out again."

He said that as if he were in the *habit* of bailing us out, which is probably precisely how he meant it to sound. It made me furious.

"By the way," said Mother, "what did you tell the detectives to get them to let us go so quickly?"

Nelson started for the door, and without looking back he said, "I told them you were working for the CIA."

"Wait a minute, Nelson!" I said so firmly that he stopped and turned around. "Why did you set my mother up in that building? Why did you want her to watch the place?"

He smiled coyly. "I didn't want her to watch the place, I wanted her to watch *him*."

"Why?" I demanded.

Nelson sighed. "Go back to Chicago, Alex." With this he left the room, closing the door behind him.

"The door swung open and a Fig Newton exited," I said.

"What in the hell does that mean?" said Peter.

"I was paraphrasing Groucho Marx."

"I mean Nelson, you twit! Why did he want Patrick watched?"

"I don't know. Him and his goddamn secrecy!" I turned to Mother and said, "He's doing it to us again! If only he'd told you what the hell he wanted you to keep your eyes open about, we wouldn't be in this mess."

"All he said was he wanted me to watch for anything unusual. But I can't believe he'd have me sit there and wait for a murder to happen."

"Don't be too sure," said Peter sardonically.

"But you said Patrick's murder is the only unusual thing that happened."

"It was."

We all thought about this in silence for a minute. Finally, I sighed with exasperation and said, "Well, one thing I do know: it looks like we're on our own now. We won't have the full force of the U.S. government behind us."

"I know. I feel safer already," said Peter.

"Nelson did make one serious mistake, and I'll bet he's regretting it now," I said.

"What's that?" Mother asked.

"He told the police we're working for the CIA, and as much as he may want us out of the picture, there's no way for him to take it back now."

"Maybe that means the police will stay out of our hair," said Peter.

"I never thought I'd see the day when there'd be trouble and we'd actually *want* the police to stay away," said Mother.

"Well, we have two leads," I said. "Derrick Holmes, the producer-director, and this Syd Wishes person, who seems to have been a friend of Patrick's. At least we know he visited him."

"I'd much rather try the actor than the director," said Peter.

"So would I, but that leaves us with another problem: Syd Wishes can't be his real name, and without it we can't hope to locate him."

"Hmm," said Mother thoughtfully, "makes you wish we still had the full weight of the U.S. government behind us."

"What about Jeff Durkin?" said Peter.

"What about him?"

"Well, maybe he knows Wishes's real name."

I thought about this, then shook my head. "I don't know, I'd rather not bring him into it if we can avoid it."

"Why not?" said Mother. "He seems harmless enough."

"Well, that's just it. Brett Lover seemed harmless enough, and he ended up dead. I wouldn't want that to happen again."

Mother made a little tsk sound and shook her head. "I hadn't thought of that. You're probably right."

Then it struck me, like a lump of hot lead dropping into my stomach. "Oh, my God!"

"What is it?" said Mother, looking at me with deep concern.

"I just realized why Patrick was killed."

"Why?" said Peter.

I looked at him. My eyes were tearing up, and I fought to keep back the impending flood. But it was hard, because I really did see the truth at last.

"Because of me," I said.

There was a stunned silence during which both Peter and mother looked at me as if I'd lost my mind. And I wish I had, because it would have made accepting what I'd just realized a lot easier to take.

"What? Nonsense!" said Mother, but her expression had changed from concern to confusion.

"It's true," I said, "think about what Nelson said: we'd jeopardized an investigation. If they really are investigating the Mob, then it's my fault that Patrick was murdered."

"How do you figure that?" said Peter, obviously distressed but trying to sound as unconcerned as possible.

"Because of my fucking big mouth!" I said loudly. "I

told him I was with the CIA because I was trying to make myself sound important! And what did he do? He *talked* about it while they were filming. And now both Patrick and the man he told about it are dead!"

Mother and Peter stared at me. Much as they would have liked to, they couldn't deny the logic of this. There was a dead quiet between us for a minute, and despite what I now believed, I really did wish they could say something to convince me otherwise. Finally Mother said, "We don't know that for a fact, darling, and even if we did know it, it was a mistake—"

"A mistake!"

She waved me off. "—and you couldn't possibly have expected this outcome. So there's no sense beating yourself until we know. Come to think of it, there wouldn't be much point in it even if we knew you were right."

"But you know," said Peter, "if what you think is true, then that makes Derrick Holmes the obvious suspect. Jeff Durkin told us Holmes *is* Mano Man Productions. If Nelson and his crew are investigating Holmes, then . . ."

His voice trailed off as he realized where that train of thought was leading. He was too kind to finish it.

"You see?" I said. "I'm responsible."

"All right now," said Mother sternly. She really has absolutely no time for self-pity or recriminations, no matter how warranted they might be. "Enough of that. We have to decide what to do now."

Further conversation was interrupted by the arrival of room service with our tea, which we automatically took out to the balcony. Preparations gave us time to think, and Mother relaxed the moment the hot cup was in her hands. We sat in prolonged silence, drinking our tea and mulling

134

over how to proceed. For my part, I was too caught up in my newfound guilt to think clearly. Mother sighed and slipped her saucer back into the cup.

"Well," she said at last, "there is one other person who might know Syd Wishes's name, and he has no connection with that video company."

"Who?" said Peter.

"Mr. Watkins. My neighbor. He seemed to know Wishes by sight—maybe he knows what his real name is."

"It's worth a try," I said. "One thing's for sure: now that we know Nelson wanted Patrick watched, we need more than ever to find somebody who knew what Patrick was up to."

TEN

Since Mother had driven her own rental car to our hotel that morning (which now seemed eons ago), we had to drive to her place in separate cars. It was almost six o'clock by the time we got there. The neighborhood was a bit busier at this hour, so the not-so-gentle sound of those suicidal palm fronds was complemented by a steady flow of traffic returning home for the day. Fortunately for us, it was still early enough to find parking spaces with relative ease.

Mother wanted to stop in her apartment to freshen up before trying Mr. Watkins. She turned the key in her door, flung it open, then threw her arms out, blocking the doorway so suddenly and dramatically that it brought to mind Margaret Rutherford as Madame Arcati.

"Someone's been in here," she said.

"How do you know?" I said.

"Can't you feel it? Somebody's been in here."

137

She dropped her arms to her sides and went cautiously into the apartment. Peter and I followed. The room looked absolutely normal. Things were not tossed around; nothing was broken; nothing was left open. Given the lack of evidence that anything was amiss, it was hard to believe that Mother was going by anything other than her feelings, and I didn't think her feelings were all that trustworthy at the moment, what with having witnessed a murder that morning.

"Mother, nothing is wrong here. What are you talking about?"

"Look!" she said, waving her arms around the room as if the disarray should be perfectly obvious.

"What?"

"Look," she said, pointing to each thing in turn, "the cushion on the couch isn't flush with the back, and the drawer in the desk over there—the second drawer—don't you see it?"

"What?"

"It's difficult to get back in correctly. There's something wrong with it. If you don't slide it in very carefully, it cocks up a little on the right."

"Well, maybe you just weren't careful the last time you used it."

"But that's just it—I don't use the desk at all."

"You don't?"

She looked at me as if I were the retarded son she'd always wanted. "Alex, what on earth would I have brought out here with me that I'd put in a desk?"

"I don't know," I said with exasperation. "Then how did you know the drawer didn't work in the first place?"

"I didn't say I didn't *try* it, I said I didn't *use* it."

"Hey, come in here," Peter called.

Mother and I followed him into the bedroom, where he stood pointing at the bed. His meaning was obvious: The bed was made neatly, but not to Mother's standards. When she makes the bed, even if it's covered with a down comforter you can still bounce a quarter off it. An attempt had been made to remake the bed, and it had fallen short.

"You know," said Peter, "whoever went through here was pretty careful."

"But not careful enough for me," said Mother.

"That's because when it comes to neatness, they didn't know they were playing with one of the big guns," I said, giving her a smile that I hoped would alleviate some of her fear. I could have saved it, because she didn't look afraid, she looked angry.

"Imagine!" she roared. "Going through my bed! What the bloody 'ell did they think they'd find in my bloomin' bedsheets!"

"Most likely they were more interested in the mattress," said Peter. Despite his concern, he was unable to hide a smile at Mother's indignation.

"Imagine!" she continued. "Not safe in me own bloody home!"

"Well, I would think you'd have realized *that* when Patrick was murdered downstairs," I said. At times like this it's important to keep things in perspective. However, it probably wasn't exactly a judicious moment to remind her of the murder. Peter looked at me and rolled his eyes, letting me know that he was thinking exactly the same thing.

"That didn't happen in my own home, young man," she said sharply, "that happened in someone else's home!"

"Well, this is it! You're not staying here anymore! You're

moving into our hotel." This is the closest I'd come to putting my foot down with my mother in a long time because with her such an action is usually ill-advised, not to mention the fact that I always sound idiotic when I do it.

"I'll not be run out of my apartment by these . . . these . . ."

"Murderers," I said flatly.

"Yes, well . . ."

"This isn't your apartment, either. It was loaned to you."

"That's as may be, but I was told I could stay here, and I'm not—"

"—going to be run out of your own home," I said along with her, "I know, I know. But you're forgetting something: Nelson told us to leave town. I assume that covers leaving this apartment."

"We told him we weren't going to go, and he didn't tell me I had to leave this place."

Her stubbornness was really starting to get the better of me. Against my better judgment, I said, "No, *I'm* telling you you have to leave this place!"

"You are?"

I swear to God, when she said that she looked just like Mary Poppins scolding the bedroom furniture. If I hadn't been so upset, I would have laughed.

"Jean," said Peter in a calm, measured tone that told both of us that he was determined to be the voice of reason, "unlike my husband here, I wouldn't think of ordering you to do anything, but you have to understand what the outcome of your staying here will be."

Peter has a talent for defusing anger by throwing combatants into total confusion.

"What?"

"I won't have a moment's rest as long as you stay here. I won't be able to sleep, because I'm sure you'll be in danger. And you and I both know that Alex won't get any rest, either. We'll probably end up having to spend every night outside on the street, watching your apartment. So for the sake of us all, please, please move into our hotel."

If Agent Nelson had spoken to us like that, we just might have left town. Of course, the years of affection among the three of us made Peter's words even more effective. Mother looked from Peter to me and blinked a couple of times, looking something like an older, more angular edition of Betty Boop. Then she sighed with resignation and said she'd pack her things.

"The one thing I can't understand is, how did they know you were here?" I said as she proceeded.

"How did they know she was *here*?" said Peter incredulously. "How did they know she was involved at all?"

"This is very strange, and not good," I said, shaking my head.

"How do you mean?" Mother asked.

"Are you kidding? I mean that with Patrick murdered, then the attempt on us, then Brett's murder, and now this break-in—I can't help feeling that whoever's doing all this is spinning out of control."

Mother paused in her packing, and for the first time she really looked uncertain. But that only lasted for a moment. Her inborn British pluck wouldn't allow her to remain unfocused for very long. She resumed packing, shrugging it off with a typically understated, "That isn't a comforting thought."

By the time she'd finished, she looked fully resigned to

moving into a luxury hotel. That's one of the things I like most about her, and one of the traits I'm most grateful she passed on to me: her ability to accept whatever comes her way, especially if it's being rolled in by a waiter.

"Anybody home?" called a voice from the landing.

"Yes! Yes, come in, Reg."

Reg Watkins came through the door. He was dressed in a tan linen suit with a yellow tie, both of which looked a little too sporty for him. He had the appearance of someone who had not lived in the city long enough to adopt its character. Although he was fairly attractive, his attire and his tentativeness gave him an air of being perpetually out of place. Mother was probably right about him being lonely. He glanced at Peter and then at me, then noticed Mother's suitcases.

"Are you going somewhere?"

Mother took on a sheepish expression and said, "I'm afraid I'm moving out."

"Oh no," he said, looking pained in a way that told me he'd already fallen under her spell. "It's the murder, isn't it?"

"Yes," she said with a sigh. "It's thrown me off more than I thought, and I really can't see staying here."

I groaned inwardly. I expected that any moment she would have a fit of the vapors and drop onto a fainting couch. Mother noticed my reaction, and from the way she narrowed her eyes for a split second, I knew I was in for it. She curled her lips and said in a tone that implied she was dealing with unruly children for whom she'd have to turn her life upside down in order to avoid a scene, "Actually, Alex won't let me stay. He thinks it's too dangerous."

She didn't know how close she was coming to being the

142

second murder victim in this complex. I really hated being forced into the role of an oversolicitous son, but she gave me no choice.

"It *is* too dangerous here," I said, hoping that my voice had conveyed that she was treading on thin ice. Unexpectedly, Watkins took my side.

"I can understand your feeling that way. Even though there's murders all over the place, you can't feel safe when it happens next door."

"Exactly my point," said Mother, her tone getting more exasperating, "there are murders everywhere, so I might as well stay here."

"No. You're coming to stay with us."

"Where do you live, Mr. Robbins?" Watkins asked, looking in my direction.

Nobody answered, and then I suddenly noticed that all three of them were looking in my direction. I turned red when I remembered that Robbins was the alias Mother had adopted for this escapade. I covered clumsily with, "Oh, I didn't realize you were talking to me. I'm, uh . . . my name is Reynolds."

"Really?" he said with a quick glance toward Mother.

"Yes," she said. "Alex is my son from my first marriage. Mr. Robbins was my second husband."

"Oh," said Watkins. I thought his eyes were about to glaze over. Then again, I thought *my* eyes were going to glaze over, too.

"So, where do you live? Is it far away?" He turned to Mother and added, "Because I'd hate to lose touch with you."

"Well, I don't . . . we don't . . ."

"What Alex is trying to say," Peter cut in, looking at

me as if he was wondering how I managed to tie my shoelaces without assistance, "is that we've just come out here to get his mother. We're from Chicago, and we're going to be going back there in a few days. Jea—" he began, then realized he didn't know whether "Mrs. Robbins" had used her own first name. "Mrs. Robbins is going to stay with us in our hotel, while we try to find a better place for her."

"Good Lord, you make it sound like I'm being packed off to a home."

"Don't tempt me," I whispered to her.

"But I think they're right," said Watkins pointedly. "If you were my mother, I'd get you out of here. I'm not sure I wouldn't insist that you went back to Chicago."

The three of us looked at him. His expression was sincere and concerned, but his words came so close to what Nelson had said to us that it gave me pause.

"What do you mean?" I said, a bit more forcefully than I'd intended.

He recoiled slightly and groped for words. "Nothing . . . nothing. I just meant . . . I know how you feel, and . . . well, I mean, what with living so far away yourselves, I imagined you'd feel better about it if she was there. I'm sorry, I didn't mean anything."

He looked so stricken that I couldn't help feeling sorry for him. I apologized, explaining that Mother's close proximity to a murder had us all on edge. He smiled as if I'd just verified what he'd been thinking.

"You see," said Mother, recovering quickly and picking up the ball, "this murder business has been a much more personal thing for my Alex."

"Really?"

"Yes. By a strange coincidence, Alex knew Patrick—the boy who was killed."

"Really?" he said, his eyes widening with amazement.

"Yes, I did. We went to college together."

"Oh," said Watkins, blushing. I realized after a moment that he was embarrassed at being so interested. "I'm really sorry." He turned to Mother and added, "Then you must have known him, too."

"No, no," she said quickly. "I didn't really know many of Alex's college friends. Alex just recognized the name when I told him about the murder." She glanced at me and raised her eyebrows. I always find it disarming that she can lie so convincingly on command, on the few occasions that she's felt it necessary to do so. It makes me wonder if I'm adopted.

"Um, listen," I said, "I was hoping to get hold of some of Patrick's other friends, and Mother said you might know one or two."

"She did?" He looked genuinely confused. "I didn't really know Patrick at all, except to talk to—say hi to. He wasn't a very . . ."

"It's all right," I said, hoping to help him along.

"I don't like to speak ill of anyone, but he wasn't a very outgoing person."

"He wasn't very friendly," I said, nodding.

Watkins looked relieved to have the onus of making a negative assessment removed from him. "Yeah. Well, I didn't know him, so I really don't know any of his friends."

"No, Mother didn't say you actually knew them, only that you recognized one—someone called Syd Wishes."

Watkins blushed again and looked down at the floor. "I recognized him, yes."

I couldn't help smiling. He looked the way I felt when that policeman caught me out about renting a porno movie. "I would have recognized him, too," I said reassuringly.

He looked up at me and some of the redness was gone. "Oh, well, yeah. He was here a few times."

"Do you happen to know his real name?"

Watkins cocked his head just slightly, "No. Why?"

"We just want to talk to him."

Watkins looked as if he'd like to ask the question again, but had decided that to do so might be considered rude. There was a confused pause during which we all glanced at one another as if carrying on some sort of ocular pub-Pong game while waiting for somebody to speak. Finally, I put on what I hoped was a look of extreme sadness and said, "Well, you see, it's just that it'd been so long since I'd seen Patrick. I just wanted to talk to somebody about how he was doing out here." Convincing lying is not one of the traits that my mother has passed on to me, so I was glad that my explanation was essentially the truth.

"Oh." His eyes looked as if they were going to glaze over again. And he didn't look like he believed me, so I guess I'm even bad at telling the near truth. "Well, I don't know what his real name is, but I know where he's going to be tonight."

"You do?"

"He's going to be at the Peacock. He's doing personal appearances there this weekend."

"The Peacock?"

"Yeah. It's a bar on Montana, a few blocks north of Ninth. He's going to be there tonight and tomorrow night. It was in the paper."

"The paper?" said Peter incredulously.

Watkins flushed again. "The local gay paper."

"Well," said Mother breezily, apparently feeling this had gone about as far as it could, "we'd better get going if we're going to go." She stopped and took hold of Watkins's small white hands. "It really was nice meeting you. I wish I could stay, but . . ." She cocked her head in my direction and raised her left eyebrow, and Watkins nodded knowingly. She added with a shrug, "Maybe I'll see you again."

"I hope so."

"Maybe we'll see you tonight?" said Peter.

Watkins looked confused for a moment; then his expression changed into something I can only describe as scandalized. "Oh, no. I'd never go to a place like the Peacock!"

ELEVEN

I'm not going to a strip joint!" said Peter.

"It's not a strip joint."

"I'm not going to a strip joint! I've been in enough of the seamy underbelly of the gay obliterati," said Peter, wrinkling his nose as if an unpleasant odor had just wafted through the car. Even at the height of irritation, he was able to coin the perfect phrase for the people with whom we'd been consorting since arriving in L.A. This rather tense exchange took place on the way back to the hotel. Mother followed in her car.

"It's not a strip joint. It's a bar."

"A bar with a stripper making a personal appearance."

"He's not a stripper, he's a porn star."

Peter looked at me as if I'd finally lost the remainder of my mind. "I really have to get you back to Chicago."

"It's not like we don't have the same kind of thing back there."

"Yeah, but we don't go to them."

"Well, we *have* to go to this one!"

Peter snorted in response.

I knew how to put a speedy end to this argument: I sighed with resignation and said, "All right, I'll go there alone."

"Wasn't last night's orgy sufficient?"

"Oh, for crying out loud!" I said, losing my patience at last. "I don't want to go either, but Syd Wishes is the only lead we have!"

He sat silently for a moment, exhaled, and then said, "After spending an evening with a bevy of beautiful boys with the morals of slugs, getting run off the road and almost killed, then seeing somebody get shot, you have to expect me to be a little cranky."

I smiled and patted his hand.

He sighed heavily again and smiled back at me. "Well, I must say, in all the years we've been together, I never realized knowing you would lead me to such an . . . interesting group of people. First the CIA, and now this."

"Look at it this way. After Derrick Holmes's party, going to a strip joint will hardly even make for a change."

We got Mother checked in to a room at our hotel, then the three of us had a quick dinner. Peter and I headed out to the bar.

Despite my protestations to Peter about the nature of the Peacock, I was relieved to find that it gave every indication of being a respectable bar, or at least as respectable as any bar can be. The building was a low-key, low-lying wood structure with a large picture window across the front. The inside of the window had been painted a flat black. On entering we were greeted by a large but pleasant man to whom we paid the requisite cover charge.

The interior of the bar was as low-key as the exterior. The walls were brighter than those of the bars I'd known in my carefree, randy youth. On one wall there was painted a large, multicolored fanlike thing, which I suppose was meant to represent the tail of a male peacock; but given the Hollywood influence, it looked a lot like the NBC logo.

Some generic techno-pop was playing loudly overhead, competing with the general noise of the crowd. In honor of the guest appearance of Syd Wishes, along with a handful of other porn stars, the place was jammed, mostly with young men, and a few old-timers like Peter and me (by that I mean people in their mid-thirties).

As with all such occasions (with the possible exception of the pretty-party) I got that feeling of comfort and safety that we all tend to experience when mingling with a herd of our own. This event was much more subdued than the pretty-party. It was more or less the type of gathering you'd find during any performer's personal appearance. The stars were dressed casually, but they were dressed. Then again, the night was young. Everyone else was as well turned out as you can be in varying combinations of denim and khaki. It was like being in an explosion at the Gap. The fans were taking the opportunity to have their pictures taken with their favorite actors, who seemed to shy away from any physical contact other than an arm over the shoulder or around the waist. It crossed my mind that despite the flagrant nature of their work, these actors realized something that the legitimate stars of today seem to have lost:

mystique is everything. I found myself admiring their marketing sense. The rest of the activities were limited to the stars autographing fig-leaf publicity pictures of themselves, which were being sold at a table near the small stage at the far end of the bar.

"This is much nicer than the type of place you usually take me to," said Peter with a playful smirk. I pinched his butt in response.

We waded through the crowd to the bar, bought a couple of rum and Cokes, and wandered away through the masses of people and tables, all the while inspecting the crowd. I think we'd both become a little wary of speaking to anyone connected with Patrick if there was a chance of being seen by anyone else who might be concerned.

We waited a long time to see if the crowd would thin out at all, but by midnight it still showed no sign of diminishing. However, our drinks did, and I really didn't want any more alcohol. We got a couple of Cokes and sat down as soon as one of the little tables was available.

I finally said, "We might as well go ahead and see if he'll talk to us." I got up and worked my way over to where Wishes was signing his name across the derrière of his own picture for a very young man who looked at him with shining eyes. Wishes thanked him and turned away, happening to catch my eye.

Syd Wishes had longish light brown hair and brown eyes that seemed to be lit from behind. His skin was clear and his face clean shaven and boyish, though I knew he must be one of the older actors since it must've been at least five years since I'd seen one of his videos. He was dressed in a white shirt and blue jeans. There was something homespun and wholesome, almost farm-boyish about him, which must have been why he was such a popular object in porn.

"Hello," he said cordially, with a pronounced drawl. When I'd seen him in a video, I hadn't noticed that he had an accent. Then again, it's hard to pick up a dialect from a groan.

"Um, hi," I said.

Wishes looked at me as if he were sure I was one of those fans who wanted more from him than he would give me (for free), and he was pro enough to deal with the situation.

"Did you want an autograph?" he said above the din. "A picture?"

"No, I was wondering if I might talk to you for a minute."

He tilted his head and flashed me an apologetic smile. "Sorry, buddy, but there's an awful lot of guys here, and I owe evahbody a little piece o'me."

I was confused for a moment, and my face must've shown it, because his excessively smooth brow furrowed.

"I mean me and my friend over there." I pointed in the direction of our table. We could just barely see Peter's head through the crowd.

"Sorry," Wishes said with a shrug and a smile that told me he couldn't help it, but he had other things to do at the moment. He started to edge away, but I put my hand on his wrist. He glanced from my hand to my face, apparently trying to decide exactly how much trouble I was going to be.

"You see," I said, trying to sound like anything other than the fans packing the place, "I was a friend of Patrick

Gleason . . . from back in Chicago. And I understand you were a friend of his, too."

"Pat?" he said, his face first brightening in recognition, then crashing as he remembered the murder. "Oh, Gawd, Pat."

He put his hand on my shoulder and steered me back to the table where Peter waited, saying, "That was really something. I still can't believe it. He was . . ."

I lost the end of his sentence somewhere in the roar of the crowd, but the look on his face told me that whatever he'd said, it was heartfelt. We reached the table and I introduced Peter. As we sat, I happened to glance in the direction of the door and my stomach dropped when I recognized a man who was in the process of paying the cover charge: It was Ren Forrest, the cameraman for Mano Man Productions. He made his way to the bar, apparently without noticing us. I nudged Peter and pointed him out.

"Well, it's too late now," he whispered loudly into my ear.

"I still can't believe it," Syd said again, oblivious to what had passed between Peter and me. He took a pack of the smoker's insignia of gaydom, Marlboro Lights, from his pocket and as he did a condom flipped out of the pocket and landed on the table. He scooped it up, a bashful smile spreading across his face as his cheeks turned a youthful pink.

"You never know when some work might come my way," he said as he stuffed it back in his pocket. He pulled a lighter from the pocket of his jeans and lit the cigarette. "I don't usually go in for a recreational slap on the ass. For me, sex is work."

154

"Sometimes it is for the nonprofessionals, too," I replied.

Peter kicked my right shin under the table.

"Do you mind if I ask where you're from?" I asked.

He blew some smoke in the air. "I'm from Houston."

"Really?"

He smiled. "We got faggots in Houston, too, you know."

There was something very straightforward and open about this guy, which really was different from the other members of his profession that I'd met in the past couple of days. There wasn't any of Patrick's pompous defensiveness, or Jeff Durkin's quality of the orphan being led astray. He didn't even exhibit any of Brett Lover's mercenary slyness. No matter what I might think of Syd's line of work, I liked him.

"I'm sorry," I said, it being my turn to blush, "I didn't mean it that way."

"S'okay," he said, tapping an ash into a cheap tin ashtray on the table. The gesture was an elegant contrast to his accent. "So, you were a friend of ol' Pat? God, he was a . . . he was . . . a nice guy."

"You sound doubtful," said Peter.

Syd batted those brown eyes of his at Peter, and his smile grew a little more sheepish. "I think he was a nice guy, deep down. You had to go a long way to see it."

"You don't have to apologize," I said. "I knew Pat pretty well a long time ago, and I'd say your assessment is pretty accurate."

"So what're you doin' here? Why'd you wanna talk to me?"

"Well . . ." I thought with this guy, probably the shortest and most accurate explanation would be the best course. "We're sort of looking into Pat's murder."

"You are?" said Syd with mild amusement.

"Alex was the one who found the body," Peter interjected.

"Jesus!" Syd said. The amusement disappeared. He looked appalled and excited at the same time.

"Yeah," I continued, "and I had to talk to the police. And from the way they acted when I was there, I don't believe they're going to do much to solve the case. They seem to think you guys don't matter."

Syd stared at me for a moment. He seemed to be trying to figure out which part of "you guys" Peter and I weren't a part of. His expression cleared quickly, and he looked like he wanted to spit. "They don't call 'em pigs for nothin'." He tapped an ash again and added, "Like my daddy used to say: I'm sure there some of 'em are good, but I wouldn't want my daughter to marry one. 'Course, he was talking about us faggots."

There was a gleam in his eye that told me he was using "us faggots" to embrace Peter and me, a sort of repayment for my "you guys" comment. It showed me that despite Wishes's rural image, he was no fool.

"So do you mind if we ask you a few questions?"

"No, siree."

I glanced at Peter, who looked back at me as if he wanted me to explain further. Even though I didn't want to, I thought we owed it to Syd to warn him.

"It's just that . . . the last two people we talked to are now dead."

Syd looked at me blankly for a minute, then shook his

head eagerly and said, "You don't have to worry 'bout me, buddy. Nobody's gonna hurt me. I'm too big."

My mind flashed back to his video before I realized that he was talking about his status as a star.

"Shoot," he said.

"Well, for one thing, how did the two of you meet? Were you in . . ."

No matter how open this guy was, I didn't know exactly how to ask him if he'd met Patrick while having sex with him. Syd seemed to notice my discomfiture, and said, "No, no, I never did him. Believe it or not, I met him a couple of years ago poundin' the pavement."

My mouth dropped open. "You mean Pat worked the streets?"

"Huh?" His face was blank for a moment. Then he laughed. "Oh no, oh no: *poundin' the pavement*. Trying to find an agent. He wanted to act, so did I. Anyway, I met him back then."

"So Pat was trying to act . . . legitimately."

Syd smiled at the word. Frankly, he flashed that denim smile at just about anything. "Sure did. Both of us tried. Pat, he did better than me. He got some work a while back, you know? Some extra work, which don't pay nothin', and a couple of little walk-on things, type of stuff that ends up on the cuttin' room floor. I don't know that he ever got anything that really panned out."

"What about you?" Peter asked.

"God's honest truth, I was already makin' videos, so there wasn't a lotta hope for me. Then there's my accent. Takes a lot of work to get rid of, and I don't know that I wanna do that. But Pat, he had a future, I think."

"Then what happened?" I asked.

"Like I says, he got some work, but not much, and didn't have anything for a long time. He didn't have no money, and he didn't have none comin' in. So . . . he did a video."

"But how did that come about? Did you get him into it?" I asked tentatively. Since I'd decided I liked this guy, I sincerely hoped he hadn't had anything to do with Patrick's downfall.

"Naw, not me. Matter of fact, he answered some ad."

"From Mano Man Productions?"

"Uh-huh," he said, nodding and taking another puff on his cigarette.

"I didn't know they advertised that sort of thing."

Syd's smile became more canny. "You don't read the right kinda newspaper, buddy."

"I see."

"The rags out here . . . they advertise in them, sometimes. So he answered this ad."

"He just answered the ad and started doing porn?"

"Well . . ." Syd said slowly, exhaling the smoke and tapping off some more ash, "it wasn't *exactly* as easy as that. It was . . ."

"What?"

"Well, let me tell ya. Look at me: I ain't got a lot of acting talent, but I got no whatcha call inhibitions, either. I mean, see, you could stick your finger up my ass right here on this table, and I wouldn't be embarrassed at all." He paused for a moment as if to make sure that I didn't want a demonstration. I demurred and he continued. "Doin' porn wasn't nothin' to me. Pat was different. He could act. I don't think he really wanted to do the videos at all."

158

"Then why did he do it?" I pressed.

Syd took a drag from his cigarette and blew out the smoke before he answered. "You know what it's like to be desperate? No, from the look of you, you don't. When I say Pat was broke, I don't mean he was down to a few thousand in the bank, I mean he was flat-out broke. So he answered the ad and went to that Holmes's place to be interviewed, with cameras rolling all the time. I don't think Pat really woulda gone through with it, but Holmes gave him some coke . . ."

"Cocaine?"

"Um-hm. Don't get me wrong—it wasn't the first time Pat did coke, and he sure as hell wasn't gonna turn down a free hit. Before he knew it, he was wasted and Holmes was fucking him up the ass."

"You mean he raped him?" said Peter, unable to hide the shock in his voice.

Syd let out a rueful laugh. "I don't know if that's exactly what you'd call it. Pat wasn't an angel, you know. Anyway, afterward, it was too late and that Holmes guy was all business."

"What do you mean?" I asked.

"Had him on tape, didn't he? Wasn't any more question 'bout whether or not Pat was going be doin' the videos, he'd already done one . . . free of charge. No turnin' back."

"Jesus!" said Peter.

Patrick nodded. "Deed was done. What was he gonna do after that? He needed money, and he'd already done his first porn. Nothing for it but to go on." He paused a moment and clucked his tongue. "God's honest truth, I don't think Pat ever got over it, though he always talked big about it. But I knew him. I knew it bothered him."

I was speechless. So it had been a lie. Patrick had lied to me again, pretending to be so damn sophisticated about his career as a porn star. It *had* affected him. I was overwhelmed with a feeling of sadness that bordered on nausea. But on the other hand, in a way I was relieved to know that he wasn't as callous as he tried to present himself. I know that sounds awful, but in a way, knowing that he'd been affected by the work reawakened my feelings for him. For the first time since our unfortunate romance, I felt a distant sense of love for him, because in all the intervening years I had sincerely believed that nothing ever touched him. I think it was at this moment, hearing this story, that all the hurt I'd felt over my relationship with Patrick finally started to heal.

"You all right?" said Peter.

I shook my head briskly to bring myself back to the present. "Yes, sure." Peter squeezed my hand and I turned back to Syd. "Tell me, have you ever done any work for Mano Man?"

Syd leaned back in his chair and clasped his hands behind his head; the smoke from his cigarette looked like it was rising from his brain. His smile reappeared. "No way, man! I'm strictly A-list. They're too new and too small."

"They're new?" Peter asked.

"Oh yeah, they just come along in the past year or so."

"What's wrong with that?" said Peter, then added quickly, "I mean from a business standpoint."

"Usually new means cheap. They don't pay well—well, none of them do, really, but new ones don't pay well at all. And they make low-grade stuff. I've gone beyond that, you know?"

"My God," Peter muttered under his breath, "they have a hierarchy."

"Tell me, Syd," I said, "have you ever heard anything . . . about Mano Man?"

He screwed up his face. "What you gettin' at?"

I glanced at Peter, then said, "Well, I guess what I'm asking is if you'd heard anything about . . . maybe Mano Man being connected to something like organized crime?"

Syd smiled at me coyly, then said, "Organized crime, eh?" He scratched his elbow, then took a drag from his cigarette, which had burned down almost all the way to the filter. "Well, I don't know about that. I'm always hearing that things like that are going on, but I don't see none of it at my end."

"Did you hear anything about it from Patrick?" I asked.

"Not that I remember in particular. But you gotta realize, he was pretty new to the business. I've been in it a while and I've learned a lot."

"Like what?"

Syd crushed his cigarette out in the ashtray and leaned in toward me.

"Like there's some things it's better not to know."

TWELVE

Before leaving the bar, Peter and I discussed whether or not to question Ren Forrest. Up until that point we had refrained from confronting anyone directly involved with the video company (after all, the actors were not exactly what you'd call regular employees) in part because we were unsure of exactly what the investigation that Nelson staunchly refused to admit was taking place entailed. Whether he was investigating the video company didn't much matter to us at this point, because the company provided the only link we knew of between Patrick Gleason and Brett Lover. We thought we might as well start with the cameraman. However, when we scanned the crowd we couldn't see Forrest for the fags. He had apparently already gone.

Peter and I left the bar and headed down the side street on which we'd parked.

"Well, that was certainly the most decent porn star I've

ever met," said Peter. It was too dark for me to see whether or not he was smiling. After a few moments had gone by without a response from me, Peter said, "Are you all right?"

"I don't think so," I said. "I think I'm really a rotten person."

Peter stopped in his tracks a few feet from a street lamp and gently tugged my arm to stop me. "Why do you say that?"

I looked down at the ground. I really was embarrassed. "Peter . . . it made me happy . . . I don't mean happy, I mean I was glad to find out that it bothered Pat to be doing porn. What a vindictive old prick I've become. That's not the reaction of a kind person."

In the dimness of that light I could see a sweet smile spread across his face, and that love I've mentioned before appeared in his eyes. "I think you're wrong," he said. "I think it's the reaction of a compassionate person. You're not glad that he was hurt, you're glad to find out he was human. Being human is a pretty good accomplishment, both for him . . . and for you."

He gave me a light kiss on the lips and we started down the street again, walking along the outside of the bar. Just after we passed the streetlight beside which we'd stopped, was a sort of alley that ran behind the bar, I suppose for deliveries and garbage pickups and the like. As we stepped beyond the wall, two men appeared from the alley and stood in front of us, one blocking Peter and the other blocking me.

"What is this?" said Peter.

Without a word, they grabbed the front of our shirts, pulling the collars tightly around our necks, and shoved us into the alley, up against the back wall of the bar. As my shoulders hit the wall I could feel the wood give way a little, and hoped that was an indication of how weak the wall was instead of how much force had been used to slam me against it. Unfortunately, the pain radiating back and forth from my shoulders to my lungs was a testament to who'd received the worst of the shock.

"You fucking faggots never give up, do ya?" said the one holding me.

The alley was hopelessly dark and I couldn't have described either of these men in anything approaching detail if my life depended on it (which was an unfortunate cliché to call to mind at that particular moment). It was like trying to make out the face of someone who was standing just outside of the lighting in a John Carpenter film. The odd thing about it was that there was something inexplicably familiar about them, and though I couldn't have sworn to it in court, I was sure these guys had been serving as guards at the pretty-party.

"What do you want?"

"You ask too many questions. We want you to stop."

"Is this a warning?" I said, choking the words out. His fist holding my collar together against my Adam's apple was making it really difficult to breathe, let alone talk.

I thought I could see the darkness of his face shift into something resembling a smile. But it could have been the pleasure in his voice that made me think that.

"We don't warn, we kill. You oughta know that by now."

With that both men reached into their respective pockets. My assailant slid his hand up in front of my face and moved his thumb; even in the general murk I could see the blade shimmer. He let out a pleased little snort and said,

"You're about to see the inside of your stomach, faggot."

The two of them pulled back the blades as if to strike, when suddenly a voice from a different quarter yelled, "Hey, what's going on?"

Both assailants' heads snapped in the direction of the voice, and we were suspended for a moment while they tried to make out who was standing there on the sidewalk, silhouetted by the streetlight a few feet back. I turned my head as much as I could, just in time to see the silhouette's arm move quickly in and out of its pocket. He yelled, "Let them go," and let off a shot into the air. Without a word the men let go of us and took off down the alley.

Peter and I slumped halfway to the ground and gasped for breath as the silhouette passed into the shadows beside us. He stuck his gun back in his pocket and helped right us.

"You okay?"

"I guess," I said, "Peter?"

"Yeah," Peter replied, rubbing his neck, "Thanks for helping us." He gasped.

"It was nothing," he replied.

We followed him out of the alley and into the light of the street lamp. I stopped abruptly in shock as I realized who our savior was.

"You're Ren Forrest, aren't you?" I said.

He nodded. "I thought I recognized you in the bar. You were at the party last night, weren't you?"

"Yeah."

In the cold light of the lamp Forrest was singularly unattractive in a pocket-protector kind of way. He looked not unlike Peter Lorre in his later years, though he was at most in his late thirties. His eyes were buggy, and even in this dim light I could tell that his black hair was greasy. I would be willing to bet he drooled while he did his job. He was the last person I'd want to have filming me having sex. That didn't come out quite the way I meant it.

"You're the cameraman for Mano Man Productions, aren't you?" said Peter.

"Videographer," he corrected.

"Sorry," said Peter demurely.

"So what was that all about?"

I glanced at Peter, then said, "I'm not sure, except that we were friends of Patrick Gleason—"

"The guy that was killed?" Forrest broke in eagerly.

His avid interest was really distasteful. I answered slowly, "Yeah, the guy that was killed."

Forrest's bug eyes rolled from me to Peter, then back to me. "Why would that have anything to do with you?"

"It doesn't," said Peter. "It's just that we've been asking a few questions about the murder, and apparently some people don't like it."

Forrest's face darkened briefly, as if a cloud had obscured the street lamp. "Yes, I can see where some people wouldn't want you asking questions about that. These aren't the kind of people who would welcome being questioned about anything."

Far from warning us, Forrest sounded almost afraid.

"Surely the police will be asking questions," I said.

"Oh, yeah, yeah." He nodded eagerly. I was surprised that his head didn't rattle. "The police have been around the company, asking questions."

"By 'around the company' I take it you mean Derrick Holmes?"

"Oh, yeah, as well as me."

"What did you tell them?"

That same dark, half-fearful look came into his eyes. He looked at me as if he couldn't quite focus and said, "There wasn't anything to tell. I don't know anything about what happened to Gleason. And I wasn't there when they questioned Derrick, so I don't know what he told the cops, though I'm sure he didn't have anything to say, either. And the police haven't been back."

I couldn't help shooting Peter a look and saying, "I told you they wouldn't pursue it."

An abbreviated smile appeared on Forrest's face. "Well, even the police know when to leave well enough alone. They know there's nothing can be done about this sort of thing. So they know when it's better to let it go. I haven't been in the business long, but I know that much."

"There are a couple of questions we'd like to ask you, though," I said.

"Yeah?"

"You were the ca—the videographer when Patrick performed with Brett Lover?"

"Yeah. I did that one. That Patrick was good." I really was afraid Forrest was going to drool. "He could keep it up for the camera. Not everyone can. Didn't go soft at all."

"I'm sure he was good at what he did," I intoned, "but that's not what I wanted to know about. Can you tell me if he said anything unusual during that filming?"

Forrest cocked his head and looked at me out of the corners of his eyes. He looked as if he didn't want to understand what I was asking.

"Like what? He didn't say much outside the script."

"Well, do you remember him saying anything about the CIA?"

"The CIA?" said Forrest loudly with a short laugh that sounded like a bark. A little bit of mucus ran out of his left nostril, and he wiped it away with his sleeve. "No, I didn't hear him say anything about the CIA! What the hell would he be saying about them? Was it a joke?"

"No," I said flatly, "it was no joke. Brett Lover told us that Patrick had said something about the CIA, I just wondered if you heard it."

"Well, Brett was *closer* to him than I was," Forrest replied with a really unpleasant leer.

"And now Brett Lover is dead," said Peter.

Forrest's eyes boggled. "He's *dead*? He's dead, too? Oh, sweet Jesus!"

He certainly looked surprised, but there was something a little overdone about the expression on his face, something behind those widened eyes of his that made me think he just might have known about Lover's death already.

"Two guys dead," Forrest continued. "If I was you guys, I'd take a hint from the police and just leave this alone!"

I glanced at Peter who was staring at Forrest through slightly narrowed eyes. "Maybe we'll do that," he said.

"You'll be safer. You don't know what these people are like." He had lost his panicked look and replaced it with a cunning smile, the meaning of which I didn't even want to know.

"Yeah, well, thanks for helping us out against those guys. You probably saved our lives," said Peter. "By the way, what were *you* doing here tonight?"

Forrest's shoulders moved in what I took to be his version of a shrug. "Just looking around. Never know when I might spot some new talent."

"Do you always carry a gun?"

Forrest rolled his eyes over in Peter's direction and said with the utmost seriousness, "Like I said, this is a dangerous business."

With that he wandered on into the darkness. We watched him go and then started back down the street toward our car.

"That is one strange dude," said Peter.

"I wonder if he was lying," I said.

"About what?"

"Well, how big a space could they have been filming in? How could he have not heard what Patrick said?"

"Maybe he left the room for a minute."

"Maybe. I'll tell you another thing that bothers me. Doesn't it strike you as incredibly lucky that he showed up when he did?"

"Incredible is the word. It was way too fortuitous," said Peter grimly.

THIRTEEN

Mother joined us for breakfast the next morning dressed in one of her trademark kimonos. It was like her to have packed a silk kimono even though she was going off to play Los Angeles lowlife. I should say lower life, because Mother is quite a striking woman, and there's only so much she can do to hide that. And there's nothing she can do to hide her accent. She looked wonderful, standing on the balcony, leaning on the railing and drinking in the morning haze as a waiter rolled in our breakfast. She was entirely in her element.

We recounted the previous evening to her over croissants with jam and tea.

"I'm not surprised at his attitude toward his work," she said after hearing our impressions of Syd. "I suppose the people who appear in these videos have to be a different sort. It's rather hard for me to understand them, but on the other hand, I guess it's all a matter of degree."

"What do you mean?" I asked.

She sighed. "Well, there's none of us without sin, as the saying goes. I just somehow feel better knowing that I've never committed any of my sins to tape."

Both Peter and I laughed at this. There was something in what she said.

"So what do we do now?" asked Mother, taking a sip of her tea.

"Well, we've lost our government connection, if Nelson is to be believed. . . ."

"I do wish you could keep the contempt out of your tone when you speak of him," said Mother.

I cleared my throat but didn't apologize. "I suppose we could track down others who've worked for Mano Man Productions, but I don't see the point. The actors seem to just be something to be used by the company. So I think if we're going to get anywhere, we have to go to the source."

"Derrick Holmes," said Peter, nodding.

"You mean you actually want to go and question him? What good would that do? Surely he's not going to tell you anything," said Mother.

I smiled at her. "No, Mother, I think it's time we tried our hand at a little breaking and entering again."

"What?"

"Well, Holmes apparently films in his house, if Jeff Durkin was telling the truth. So we should probably start there."

"We *can't* break into a Malibu home," said Mother with a look on her face that said she was trying to be aghast at the suggestion. It would have been more effective were it not for the fact that on our first case we'd broken into a hotel room. Of course, we'd been given a key to accomplish that one by a hotel employee who happened to be a friend of ours, but it was still breaking and entering. Far from a foolish act, it had actually proven to be a wise move.

"Why not?"

"For one thing, I don't see what good it will do. Surely he wouldn't leave evidence that he murdered two people lying about."

"Yeah, but he might leave some evidence that he's involved with the Mob lying about, and that would be just as good. We might find something that Nelson and his people have been looking for. At least it would get Holmes put away."

"I won't even bother arguing the legality of that," said Mother with a sidelong glance at me. Then she went back to her argument, "For another thing, there'll probably be somebody there. How would we be sure that we could do it without being discovered. Lay in wait outside his house till we see him leave?"

"I have a little idea about that."

"What?" said Peter, narrowing his eyes at me.

I laid my hand against his cheek. "Sweetheart, I think you oughta be in pictures."

"This is the worst idea you've ever had," said Peter disconsolately as we climbed out of the car. We'd parked at the end of the street so that we could approach Holmes's house without being seen.

"All we need you to do is keep whoever's home—if there is anyone home—busy for a few minutes while we look around. It'll be easy. After all, Holmes told you he was interested in having you in his videos."

" 'Having me' being the operative word."

"You'll be perfectly all right. We only want to look around for a few minutes."

Peter stopped and defiantly put a hand on his hip. But he was smiling. "You know, it really gives me pause the way you offer me up like this . . . like some sort of human sacrifice."

I curled my lip at him. "You're not in any danger, my dear. If memory serves, they can only sacrifice virgins."

"Not these people."

"We only need you to string him along for a little while."

"I must say you have a pretty cavalier attitude toward dangling me like a piece of meat in front of a hungry wolf. Remember what happened to Patrick Gleason when he played at auditioning for this guy. Before he knew it, he'd made a video."

"Just don't put anything up your nose. Or any other orifice, for that matter."

"I don't think you comprehend the danger of being compromised you're putting me in," Peter said with the measured primness he'd learned from years of living with my mother.

"Oh, it won't come to that," said Mother, getting a little weary of this discussion as we approached our prey. "If things start to get out of hand, I'll rescue you."

"How?"

"Don't worry about it," she said, waving him off.

"How?" said Peter, turning to me.

"Don't worry—she really does have a good idea, but it'll work better if you don't know about it."

"Cheer up, luvey—he might not even be home!"

I couldn't help but notice that Mother's eyes were shining and her step purposeful. I was reminded once again of how much our lives had changed in the past year or so, since we'd given up our placid former lives to become part-time agents. Mother is uniquely suited to our new line of business: not everyone's parent is so exhilarated at the thought of breaking into a house.

A tall wooden fence stood along the left of the house, so the deck and pool couldn't be seen from the street. A small walk of paving stones led to a gate in the fence. At first I thought that this was so the pool could be accessed without going through the house, but once we reached the gate, I realized it was meant only as an exit, since there was no handle on outside. Mother and I ducked into a recess between the gate and the house while Peter went to the front door. He rang the bell and waited while we listened. After a moment, the door opened. We couldn't see Holmes, but I recognized his voice. His tone was devoid of surprise at Peter's arrival, as if it were inevitable that anyone in whom Holmes expressed an interest would be drawn back to him. It gave me chills. Peter mumbled something about how he'd thought it over, and decided he'd like to do some videos. At least he thought he would. Holmes stepped just partially into view, put a hand on Peter's shoulder and guided him into the house. The door closed behind them.

"Let's go!" I said quietly.

Mother pulled a nail file out of her bag and slid it between slats in the gate. She caught the latch on the opposite side, pushed the file up, and gently pulled the gate open. Once again I found it disarming that she was so adept at this sort of thing.

"Thank God you're on our side," I whispered.

She flashed a smile over her shoulder, then opened the

gate a crack and peeked in to make sure none of Holmes's entourage was lolling by the pool. She signaled me that the coast was clear; we stepped through the gate and I closed it quietly behind us.

Once inside, she straightened up at the sight of the deck and pool and said, "Coo, this is lovely."

"We're not sightseeing, Mother!"

"But it is! I could just see myself sitting over there on that deck chair of an afternoon. Of course, I'd have to find a houseboy to bring me Mai Tais."

"I think the house comes with one. Now, will you focus! We've got to get to it!"

Fortunately, the living room, through which Peter and I had entered for the party, faced the ocean, so we were relatively safe for the moment. French doors stood open immediately to our right, and we edged quietly toward them, keeping close to the house, Mother leading the way. Once again she peeked around the corner, then waved over her shoulder for me to follow her in.

We found ourselves in a huge bedroom. A large square mirror hung in a frame on the wall directly across from the French doors, and I was momentarily startled by my own reflection as I came in. The walls were a muted tan; the carpet felt expensive. A small desk stood under a window to the right of the French doors. There was a long, low six-drawer dresser along the wall facing the bed, and matching nightstands on either side of the bed. The bed itself was king-sized, but the room was more than big enough to accommodate it without looking cramped. The most startling thing in the room was a video camera mounted on a tripod, which stood in one corner. I grimaced when I saw it. It immediately came to mind that the sleazy Mr. Holmes probably enjoyed making movies in his own bed. Then again, a lot of people like to work in bed.

The door leading to the interior of the house was open, and we could hear Holmes and Peter talking. The living room was separated from the bedroom, but we could still hear their conversation, even though they were speaking in normal tones. A normal tone for Holmes was that same low, coaxing voice that he'd used on us at the party. Holmes was conducting a sort of interview, asking Peter in the friendliest way possible about his sexual background: whether he slept with both men or women, how much he enjoyed it, which he enjoyed more, and several other questions so personal that I wouldn't have discussed them with my proctologist. Peter was delivering his answers with just the right combination of embarrassment and false bravado. We listened for a moment to try to make sure there was nobody else around, then Mother said:

"You take the dresser, I'll take the desk."

She started for the desk, but I grabbed her by the elbow and said as forcefully as I could while still remaining quiet, "Oh, no, you don't! The last time we searched a room, I ended up rifling through someone's unmentionables. You take the dresser this time."

Mother smiled at me cryptically, said, "Very well," and headed for the dresser.

I went to the desk and opened each drawer in turn, finding absolutely nothing out of the ordinary. I don't know what I expected (actually, neither Mother nor I knew exactly what we were looking for, but that didn't mean we shouldn't look), but I expected something less mundane than cheap envelopes and paper clips. The desk was filled with the innocuous things you'd expect to find in anybody's office. Not so much as a dirty picture.

As I worked on the desk, I glanced over to see what Mother was doing and was surprised to see her going through the dresser with such cool efficiency, it made me wonder if just maybe she'd been practicing over the years with my own dresser at home. That wasn't a comforting thought. She slipped her hands between stacks of underwear as clinically as if she were checking Holmes for a hernia.

I closed the last desk drawer just as Mother was finishing with the dresser. She looked over at me and shrugged, and I returned the gesture.

At that moment we heard Holmes out in the living room laugh briefly and clap his hands together. The sound was so unexpected that we moved closer to the door and listened. Apparently Peter had successfully passed the interview portion of the program. What Holmes said next threw me into a panic.

"Okay, so if you're . . . comfortable, I'd like you to take off your clothes. Slowly."

"Now?" said Peter.

"Uh-huh."

"My God," I said to Mother, "we've got to get him out of there."

"He's got lots of clothes—let's finish the room."

"No!" I said, and for a moment I was afraid I'd said it too loudly. We listened for a minute, but all we heard was a shuffling, then Holmes saying, "That's right . . . just like that. Hmm. Good upper body."

"Hurry up," I said.

The only thing left were the nightstands, each of which had only one drawer. I went to the one on the left of the bed; Mother went to the right. We glanced at each other, then slid the drawers open. In mine there were two publications: a phone book, on top of which lay an X-rated video catalogue from a company called Admiral General Distributors.

"Oh my God!" said Mother in a breath.

I slid my drawer shut and looked at her. Her face had completely drained of color. She was staring down at the contents of the drawer as if she'd discovered a tarantula. But I knew it couldn't be anything as innocent as that, or she would have just closed the drawer. As it was, she seemed paralyzed.

"What is it?" I said excitedly.

She didn't speak or look up, she merely motioned for me to come over there.

I crossed around the bed to her side and looked over her shoulder. There was a gun lying in the front of the drawer, but that wasn't what had made Mother exclaim. Beside the gun was a small leather folder about the size of a wallet. It looked faintly familiar. She reached down into the drawer, extracted it, and flipped it open.

"What is that?" I said.

She looked over her shoulder at me. The color had returned to her face, and she no longer looked shocked; she looked angry.

"What do you think?" She held it up for me to see. Now I knew why she was angry. She closed it, replaced it, and quietly slid the drawer shut.

I crossed back to the bedroom door just in time to hear Holmes say, "Turn your back to me while you take that off.

That's good. Now turn around." My stomach flipped at the thought of him looking at Peter. I said to Mother, "Go! We've got to get him out of there!"

She hurriedly slipped out through the French doors, while I glued my ear to the goings-on in the living room. Holmes was making remarks about Peter's physique that made me want to strike him repeatedly about the head with a tire iron. I was ready to curse my mother for taking so long, but reminded myself that she'd only left two seconds ago.

Suddenly Holmes said, "All right, now—if you're still with me here, we can do a screen test. We'll have to go into my bedroom for that."

At that I almost froze, but I managed to thaw enough to slip out the French doors before Holmes and Peter entered the hallway, from which they certainly would have been able to see me. I stayed just outside the doors, though, for fear something would go wrong with Mother's plan. If it came to that, I was going to have to rush in, whatever it might do to our investigation. But frankly, after what we'd just learned I would have liked to blow everything wide open then and there.

I heard them come into the bedroom. There were a couple of minutes of silence while Holmes arranged the video camera at the foot of the bed. Then he said, "All right, now I want you to crouch on the bed, hands and knees, leaning slightly backward."

Fortunately, before Peter submitted to this further indignity, the doorbell rang. "Fuck!" said Holmes loudly. For a moment, I was really, really afraid that he was going to decide to just ignore the bell, but it continued to ring, accompanied by a pounding on the door. He finally said in a calmer tone, "I better get that. Just wait here a minute."

I heard Peter say, "Shit"; then a commotion advanced from the living room to the bedroom.

"Where is he?" yelled Mother at full tilt, "where is my son?" Apparently she had reached the bedroom, because when she suddenly yelled, "Good God!" she was very near the French doors.

"Lady, what the hell do you think you're doing?" said Holmes loudly, but his voice rang hollow. It sounded as if he was used to scenes.

"Get up!" she roared, her voice heavy with scorn and indignation. "Get up and get out of here! To think I raised you and this is what you've come to! You're coming with me."

"Mother . . ." Peter stammered uncertainly. We'd been right not to brief him about our plan beforehand. His shock and surprise were entirely believable. "Mother . . . how did you know I was here?"

"Jamie told me," Mother exclaimed, and I wondered exactly where she'd pulled that name from. We'd never known anyone by that name.

"Jamie?" said Peter, his bewilderment sounding exactly right.

"Yes, and you should be glad he did! We're getting out of here. And you!" Apparently she was turning on Holmes. "You should be ashamed of yourself. Pandering. *Pandering*, that's what you're doing! Pandering to the lowest common denominator! You should be more than ashamed of yourself, you should be in jail!"

"We weren't breaking the law here, lady. Behind closed doors and all that," Holmes replied with a weary tone that sounded curiously amused.

Mother made a snarling noise, and then said, "Let's get out of here, young man! And if you ever come back, I'll let your father know about it, and then see what happens to you!"

Their voices had faded away as she'd said this, and I took it to mean that they were on their way out of the house. I beat a hasty retreat through the gate, closing it as quietly as I could, and up the street. I got in the car and watched as Mother pulled Peter down the street by his ear, presumably keeping in character in case they were watched as they left. Peter had managed to slip on his shorts, but nothing else. He clutched the remainder of his clothing over his crotch.

When they reached the car, Mother opened the door and shoved Peter in, climbing in after him. She started the motor and did a three-point turn so that we could leave without driving past Holmes's house.

"What I want to know," said Peter irritably as he struggled back into his clothes, "is why I always end up naked on these cases! First time out it was those goddamn Russians, this time *you* watch a porno movie and *I* end up doing a striptease for that pervert!"

"My little Mata Hari," I said, tousling his hair. He bristled, so I knew he really was angry, not just playing.

"And he sure seemed to find the whole thing amusing, though I don't know why. He had this disgusting smile pasted on his face all the time I was . . . I felt like I was being toyed with."

Trying to quell his anger, I said, "You didn't let him toy with you, did you?"

"For God's sake, do you know how I felt stripping for that ape?"

"Like you were serving your country?" I replied, still trying to lighten the mood. He snorted at me. I knew he must feel humiliated, but it was important to keep in mind that it was for a good cause, even if it wasn't exactly national security.

"Next time, *I'm* going to search the room, *you're* going to do the striptease."

"Peter," Mother cut in, "you might take some time to realize it, but it really was for a good cause."

This brought him up short a bit. He stopped fuming and looked at her. "Did you find something?"

Mother glanced at me in the rearview mirror, and what we'd found in Holmes's room suddenly sprang back to my mind. Mother's expression matched exactly what I was feeling: extreme distaste.

"What did you find?" Peter prompted.

"The last thing we were expecting," said Mother.

"What?" Peter demanded, getting irritated with our hedging.

"We found an ID," said Mother, a measure of bitterness in her tone.

There was a slight pause; then Peter said, "An ID? What kind of ID?"

"A little card in a leather case," mother replied, curling her voice along with her lips, "a badge along with a picture ID card."

"What are you talking about?"

I explained through clenched teeth, "It was an ID for a man named Scott Keller of the FBI. But the picture on the card was of your friend the ape, Derrick Holmes!"

"*What!*"

"Yes, my darling husband," I said wryly, "the Mob behind Mano Man Productions is *our government.*"

FOURTEEN

We didn't even bother with a stop at our hotel. We headed straight to the Beaumont to confront Agent Lawrence Nelson. Mother called him from the lobby, and when she got off the phone she said that he'd reluctantly agreed to see us, and that we could come up to his room. She also said that if he was surprised, he didn't give any indication of it. I'm sure that comes from years of practice at that irritating stoicism of which I'm sure he's proud. However, at that point I was so furious I was determined to rattle his pillar whatever it took.

We went up to his room on the fourteenth floor and I knocked on the door, which opened almost before my knuckles had recoiled. Nelson ushered us in with his usual professional proficiency, which pissed me off even more. Then again, I'm sure he uses his professionalism to irritate people on a regular basis. We would have declined to sit, if he'd offer us a seat.

"I told you I wouldn't be able to help you if you continued in this investigation of yours," he said, as if he were opening and closing this meeting at the same time. I would have loved to have smacked him, but I had a feeling my fist would bounce off him. I would have yelled at him, but I was pretty sure my voice would bounce off him, too. I decided on a different tack.

"Well, Larry, we don't need any help," I said, wrapping my tongue around his name like it was a hard thing in a hamburger. I hoped it sounded as distasteful to him as it felt to me. "You see, our investigation is going quite well—isn't it Peter?"

"Oh yes, very well," said Peter, entering into it with me.

"In fact, we're really getting good at ferreting things out. Like that guy Holmes."

I paused and watched Nelson, but there wasn't so much as a twitch.

"Sherlock Holmes, I mean," I added with a smile. "You know, you'd be surprised what a couple of faggots can do when they set their minds to it, isn't that right?"

"A couple of faggots and a mother," my mother added.

"Yeah, you should get some more of us working for you, Larry. There's no telling how much public-spirited faggots will do for their country—assuming they know what they're doing and who they're working for."

I have to admit here that I was beginning to enjoy myself. I felt like Lucy Ricardo trying to get the Palace guard to laugh. The stillness that descended around Nelson was almost Zen-like, and I knew it must have been costing him something, though he didn't show it.

"Of course," said Peter, taking up the thread, "I suppose if you were to use some more gays, it'd be the same way you use us. They'd *know* they were working for you, though, wouldn't they?"

Nelson's expression still didn't change. He turned to me and said, "I assume you'll be getting to the point soon."

I had that killer feeling you get when someone jostles you in the subway. I made an effort to control myself.

"Well, our investigation has led us in some interesting directions, and we've reached a point where we thought you could be of some help."

Nelson replied calmly, "Once again, I've told you that I can be of no further help to you."

I leaned in toward him and said, "Oh, I think you can. There's just a few little things you might be able to explain to us."

His only response was a raised eyebrow. Even that ticked me off.

"For example, why is the FBI running a gay porn company?"

"Are they?" he replied simply.

There it was again, that imperturbable attitude of his that makes me want to slap him with a dead fish. He didn't move.

"You know damn well they are," I said angrily, at the same time telling myself that losing my temper with Nelson was never the way to get to him. "And I can guess what they're up to!"

"Hmm," he said. "Then why did you need to see me?"

"Larry," said Mother, her tone calm but firm enough to let him know she meant business, "I think it's about time you told us what's going on."

Nelson's head pivoted in her direction. "Your son seems to know what's going on. Perhaps *he* can explain."

"I can explain it, all right!" I said. "Your little boys in blue suits set up a porn company of their own to get the inside track on the organized crime connection, isn't that it? That's how they're conducting their investigation, isn't it?"

"Is that true?" Mother asked.

"I told you before that I couldn't discuss an investigation in which you are not involved. You're not involved in this investigation."

"Oh yes we are," said Mother, getting angry now herself. "Patrick's death got us involved, and the murder of that other young man—"

"Brett Lover," Peter chimed in.

"Yes, Brett Lover," Mother continued. "That got us even more involved. That young man died because he was coming to talk to us. We couldn't be more involved if we'd hung out a shingle."

Despite the tension in the room, Peter and I both glanced at her when she spat out this mixed metaphor. She really did come out with the most extraordinary things at the oddest times.

"You know what I mean," she said primly.

I turned back to Nelson and said, "Look, we've worked for you in the past, and you know that you can trust us."

He pointed his face at me. He didn't smile, but he looked as if he would have liked to. "The way I could trust you not to tell anyone you were working for the government?"

So he knew about that.

"It was a slip," I said feebly.

"It was a slip that may have destroyed an operation."

I figured I should use the opportunity to turn a weak

defense into a decent offense. "So you *have* set up a gay porn company."

A very curious expression came over Nelson's face. "I'd be very interested to know what makes you think the government is involved in such a thing."

Peter replied, making very little attempt to hide his contempt, "We happened upon an ID card. A card that belongs to one of your people."

"One of *my* people?"

"One of the government's people," said Mother, "who's going by the name of Derrick Holmes."

There was an uncharacteristic hesitation on the part of Nelson. "How did you happen to find this ID card?"

Mother beamed her most charming smile at him. "We broke into his house and searched it."

"You *what*?" Nelson exclaimed, forgetting himself for the first time in our not-too-long and none-too-happy acquaintance.

Bingo! I thought. I felt a great sense of accomplishment. You *can* squeeze something out of a turnip: if not blood, at least a reaction.

"Peter served as our decoy. While he kept Holmes busy, we slipped in at the back of the house and searched it."

"What in the hell do you mean by doing something like that?" said Nelson hotly.

Peter shrugged. "We work for the government."

"Christ!" said Nelson, clearly making an effort to control himself. "I should have *sent* you back to Chicago!"

"How would you have done that, Larry?" I said. "In a box?"

That was all it took to get him to turn on me. His olive skin took on a reddish cast. "Do you have any idea what you may have done? Do you realize that this is not a *game* you're intruding on? It's a federal investigation that's taken months and months to set up. I might add that it's a federal investigation that's cost a lot of money and manpower, and your continued intrusion is likely to destroy what we've worked for. And then you come blundering into the middle of it as if you're doing nothing worse than crashing a party, and throw all that work out the window!"

I didn't respond right away. I wanted his words to hang in the air for a moment so he'd have a chance to think about them. Perhaps because we work for him, I like to think that Nelson has some idea of the value of human life, but he is purposely vague and obscure about most things, so you never really know where he stands. Anyone who reads the papers knows that these government people can have, to put it nicely, a rather deviant set of values. And unfortunately, thanks to our discovery at Holmes's house, I had a pretty good idea of how much value they put on gays.

"This investigation that you say we've harmed so much—it *does* include running Mano Man Productions, doesn't it?" I asked.

Nelson looked at me for a moment. He'd regained his composure somewhat, and his eyes took on the sharp incisiveness with which I was uncomfortably familiar. He looked like he'd caught me in something. "I'm not part of that investigation," he said with quiet firmness.

"Oh, come on, Nelson!" said Peter. "Don't you think when you're caught in the act you should take it like a man?" I noticed Peter's smile and if I hadn't been so angry with Nelson I would have laughed. As always, Peter had chosen his words carefully: nothing would be more ironic to Nelson than being accused of unmanliness by one of us.

190

However, Nelson chose to remain unshaken. He returned a little smile of his own and repeated, "I am not part of that investigation."

This really did bring me up short, because I knew he was telling the truth. Whatever else I may think of him, I believe that he's *intrinsically* honest; otherwise, we really never could have worked for him. He may stretch the truth at times, but Nelson would rather dance around the truth by omission than tell an out-and-out lie. When he said he wasn't mixed up in that investigation, he was probably giving the letter of the truth but not the spirit of it (a subtle difference that he'd been known to use on us on occasion). I had the feeling if we hit on the right question, we'd get answers.

"I haven't lied to you," he added.

"No, but you're a master of expedient truth," said Peter, the right corner of his mouth turning down.

We stood for a moment, the three of us staring at the one of him. After what seemed like an eternity, Nelson took a deep breath and addressed us:

"But let's say, Alex, that your earlier speculation was . . . somewhat accurate. Say that a branch of the government, other than my own, was involved in a probe of the connection between the porn business and organized crime. If I saw that you were stumbling into that and threatening to throw a monkey wrench into the investigation, don't you think it would be my duty to stop you?"

"Hypothetically," I said, and I could feel my cheeks burning, "if your idea of an investigation is to further exploit credulous young gay men, you couldn't *stop* me from throwing a monkey wrench into it."

Nelson turned his eyes to the floor, then rolled them

back up at me in that well-oiled way of his. You simply can't imagine Nelson squeaking. He replied with unruffled intensity: "Do you think for a moment that if those young men were not working for Mano Man Productions, they wouldn't be working for another company of the same . . . ilk?"

"That's not the point, and you know it!" I yelled.

"Alex, please," said Mother in a tone that implied I wasn't helping matters. I didn't care.

"I believe that the investigation is very important. I'm sure you believe that it's important to stop organized crime. Surely you don't want the Mob exploiting your people."

"I don't want the government doing it, either," I snapped.

He continued slowly, "I realize that young men are being . . . used"—it pleased me that he couldn't think of a less volatile word for it—"as a means to an end."

"As a means to *your* end," I said, not wanting to let him off the hook. "For God's sake, Nelson! We went to the party Mano Man threw—drugs were being passed around in candy bowls!"

"If you're going to infiltrate an organization, you have to become part of it."

"But *you're* not becoming part of it—you're sending other people in for you."

To my surprise, Nelson looked somewhat abashed, though I don't know why it surprised me. Even though I don't like him, I can't deny that Nelson is a very straight arrow, in every sense of the term. Until we found Holmes's ID card, I never would have believed that Nelson would have been involved in anything that would exploit an American citizen, regardless of sexual proclivities.

The blush that had spread over his cheeks earlier faded a bit. He continued to look me in the eye—he was courageous enough not to turn away in the face of defeat—and said, "The fact that some young men are being used is an unfortunate by-product of that operation. But you have to remember that they are performing *willingly*."

"That's not what I hear," I said. This seemed to take Nelson by surprise. Or at least, his expression changed to something I didn't recognize, and I took it to be surprise.

"What do you mean?"

I told Nelson the story of how Holmes had literally screwed Patrick into the business.

The redness disappeared from Nelson's cheeks completely, and he didn't look like he believed us. But he didn't say anything.

Peter folded his arms across his chest and raised one eyebrow at our unresponsive employer. "We have it from a source who has no reason to lie to us." The implication was perfectly clear to Nelson, judging by the glance he shot Peter.

"That's very interesting," he said, in an oddly hollow tone.

"Now, Larry," said Mother, "let's unhypothetical this for a minute. I've always heard that organized crime is involved in pornography, but not how it works." She narrowed her eyes at him, and a sly smile played around the corners of her mouth. "Obviously they're not the ones *making* the videos. Where do they come into it?"

Offering Mother any sort of explanation was tantamount to giving us more ammunition with which to continue our investigation, and that was the last thing Nelson wanted us to do. But when he looked from my mother to me, I could see him relenting. I knew it was because of what we'd told him about Holmes's use of Patrick.

To my amazement, he actually smiled. This, I was soon to realize stemmed from his having decided on a way to answer Mother that satisfied all areas of his conscience.

"I prefer to let things remain in the realm of the hypothetical," he said.

I groaned; Mother sighed and threw up her hands in exasperation. Peter continued to glare at Nelson.

"But—still purely in the hypothetical—if *I* were in organized crime, I would set up a company that would . . . to some extent . . . monopolize the marketing aspect of the business. Let's say you wanted to make pornographic videos. You could do that, but ultimately you'd have to get them out to the stores through my company. Similarly, the stores that wanted the videos would have to deal with my company."

"A distributorship," said Peter.

"And would that company hypothetically be called Admiral General Distributors?" I asked sharply.

Nelson looked directly into my eyes. I think he was surprised that we'd learned this. Surprised, and maybe a little impressed. "That would be as good a name as any."

"So that's who you guys are investigating," I said, realizing as I said it that I was being injudicious.

He replied with a heavy sigh, "As I've said before, I'm not involved in their investigation." It almost escaped me that he had put the slightest emphasis on the word "their." That really puzzled me, because I had the feeling he was trying to tell us something in his usual discreet, indirect, infuriating way. "Of course you must realize that the CIA and the FBI do not normally work together."

"Then what is your investigation? Why are you out here?" said Mother, sounding as if she were at the end of her tether.

Nelson thought for a moment, then appeared to have arrived at the most forthright way to answer without giving any real information at all. "I'm on a case involving diversion of funds, nothing more."

Now I really was confused. "But I don't understand. If you weren't working together, how did you know we'd blundered"—I realized what I was saying and corrected myself—"how did you know we'd happened into the FBI's operation to begin with?"

"Your mother—" Nelson began to reply, but I cut him off.

"I know that part of it; I mean, how did you know there was an operation going on out here at all if it wasn't yours?"

Nelson looked at me with absolutely no expression on his face and replied: "Kismet."

Now I knew how Jean Arthur felt when that damn mink coat fell on her head. "That's really funny, Nelson. Apparently you don't know how serious this is."

He leaned toward me. "Oh yes, I do," he said with quiet intensity. "It's you who don't. You have no idea how much danger you're in."

"From whom?" I snapped. "The Mob or the government?"

The rest of the conversation played out like a repeat of the first one we'd had with Nelson in L.A., the only exception being that all four of us were a damn sight more irritable about the whole thing. Nelson told us we were in the way and should leave town; we told him he couldn't pay us to leave now, at least not until we discovered who had killed Patrick and Brett. When we left Nelson I felt drained and exhausted.

"Well, *that* was enlightening," said Mother.

"In what way?" said Peter. I was glad he'd said it. He sounded less petulant than I would have.

"Well, for example, you know that Nelson, for all that he is, would never betray a trust. But that 'hypothetical' claptrap was obviously his way of confirming that we were right, while preserving secrecy."

"And you think that's noble?" I said, a little more sharply than I would usually speak to my mother.

"I think nobility takes many different forms. So, yes, I think Nelson was being noble—or at least, he was trying to treat all sides fairly. Now, second," she went on before either of us could comment, "I don't think it was just my imagination that he was distressed at the idea of using those boys in those videos."

Boy, I hated to admit that one. But truth to tell, he'd given me the same impression, too. Peter grudgingly admitted as much with a reluctant, "I guess so."

"Look," I interjected, eager to poke some holes in Nelson's halo, "he may be telling us the truth about that idiot case of his, but I still don't believe that's why he came here. He flew out to get rid of us."

"Yes, you're probably right," said Mother, but she didn't look happy about it. Her tone surprised me, and I wondered for a moment at the frustration on her face.

"What is it?" I said.

"Nothing, darling. I'm just wondering if we haven't hit a wall we won't be able to pass. Not with the government and maybe the Mob against us."

"You don't want to give up, do you?"

"Not with two men dead," she replied with resolve, "but if our own people stonewall us—I mean the CIA— then I don't see how we're going to proceed."

I thought about that for a moment, afraid that she might be right. Then an entirely different thought struck me.

"That's another thing I don't understand," I said, wrinkling my forehead.

"What?"

"Well, if Mano Man Productions is being run by the government as a way into organized crime, so what? That doesn't explain why Patrick was killed."

"I don't understand, dear."

"What I mean is, we thought that Patrick was killed because he mentioned that one of his friends was with the government while they made their video. But with what we know now, that doesn't make any sense."

"Why not?" Peter asked.

"Well, of the three people at the video session, Patrick and Brett are dead. And that leaves Holmes."

Peter interrupted with, "If Ren Forrest was telling the truth about not having heard what Patrick said. And that's a big 'if.' "

"But that aside, if Holmes is working for the government I can't see why he would kill them. I mean, what difference would it make to anybody who was there when he said it?"

The three of us pondered this for a moment and then

Mother said, "Unless he told somebody else about you that we don't know about."

An idea suddenly came to me, and it was one I didn't like. "Oh, my God," I said.

"What is it?" Peter asked.

I turned to him and replied, "I wonder how many people are present when you make a video."

FIFTEEN

There were two possible resources for the information we needed: Derrick Holmes, whom I didn't think we dared approach at this point, and Jeff Durkin, whom I was reluctant to approach for fear of getting him killed. But we didn't have much of a choice.

Jeff lived in West Hollywood, the "boys' town" of the L.A. area, on a side street called Sherman Avenue just off Santa Monica Boulevard. Unlike the jungle foliage–lined street on which Patrick Gleason had lived and died, Sherman Avenue was relatively open to the sun, in a "stranded in the desert" sort of way. It seemed to be suffering from the worst type of glowing haze: it was bright in a hot, dusty, skin-roasting way that beat down so hard on the buildings that they seemed to be crumbling under the weight. The effect was of brightly lit decay. The street was lined on both sides with cars, all of which belonged in the front yard of some backwoodsman with more children than teeth. We parked directly behind a dark blue Volkswagen Bug with empty food cartons piled from floor to ceiling in the backseat. It made the name "Bug" conjure up some rather unfortunate visual images.

Jeff's apartment was in a small, flat L-shaped building that looked like a stucco version of the Bates' Motel. It was painted the color of putrefied algae. According to one of the peeling labels on the line of broken mailboxes, Jeff Durkin lived in number 8, which was in the armpit of the "L."

The three of us walked carefully along the cracked walkway that ran the length of the building, cautious lest we slip and slide on the moss that seemed to be growing out of the concrete instead of over it. The door to Jeff's apartment bore five long, vicious cracks running diagonally down from the peephole to the doorknob. They looked like they'd been left there by Freddy Krueger. Some indecipherable overproduced pop music was blaring from inside.

I knocked on the door and we waited, but there was no answer. I figured it must be really difficult to hear over the music, so I knocked again, louder, with my fist. After a minute, the music suddenly dropped to nothing and the door flew open.

Jeff stood there, naked but holding a washcloth over his crotch, which I figured was his idea of modesty. He looked startled for a moment before he recognized us and smiled. Then he noticed Mother. "Oops, just a minute." He disappeared back into the apartment.

"If I'd ever answered the door like that, my mum

200

would've skinned me for sure," said Mother, her eyebrows slightly raised and a doubtful smile playing about the corners of her mouth.

Peter turned his most winning grin on her and replied, "If you'd answered the door like that you would've looked like a Botticelli."

Her smile broadened as she narrowed her eyes at him. "I don't know exactly what you mean by that, but it's the type of thing that makes me glad you love my son."

Jeff popped back in the doorway, having thrown on a pair of jeans and a sleeveless black T-shirt. "Hi, sorry, I was just getting cleaned up . . . out of the shower."

"It's okay," I said. "Can we talk to you for a minute?"

"Sure, sure. Come in," he said. He walked into the apartment, which we took as our cue to follow.

The inside of his apartment made Patrick's look like a palace. The floor was solid cement, the middle of which was covered with a really frightening throw rug, and that's not just coming from the perspective of someone stereotypically supposed to have some interior design sense. Even if I were straight, I'd have found that rug frightening.

"Eau de Mold," Peter whispered to me. I nodded. It really did smell as if mud had settled like squatters in the corners of the room.

There was a little round table sitting against one wall, and a tiny portable television sat on it along with a boombox that had presumably been the source of the noise. The only other piece of furniture in the place was a couch, which looked like it had been upholstered with the coat of a recent immigrant. Mother, Peter, and I sat on it gingerly (I could've sworn a puff of dust flew up from it as we came to rest), and Jeff pulled up a folding chair that had one broken leg.

He said, "I can't get you anything because I don't have anything—except some red wine. Unless . . . would you like some wine?"

We all declined graciously.

"So what did you wanna talk about?"

"Well," I said, taking the lead, "I was wondering: the day that you . . . filmed with Patrick—the day he was killed—was anybody else there?"

"Oh, sure!" he said ingenuously. "Lots of people."

I'd gone beyond the point of being shocked by these guys, especially by Jeff, who unlike Patrick wasn't purposely trying to shock me. That's what made it so sad. It wasn't his fault. It wasn't that Jeff had lost his values; it was more like his education had stopped before reaching the "V"s.

"Who?" I asked.

He shrugged. "Everybody that was gonna work. There were five or six guys—they were doin' an awful lot of filming that day."

"Actors?" said Peter.

Jeff nodded.

I thought about this for a moment, but I just couldn't believe that anyone from the Mob would be actively participating in the videos.

"Was anybody there who wasn't actually in the videos? I mean anybody who was just there?"

Jeff's angelic face clouded over as if the energy that lit it was needed elsewhere in order for him to remember. After a moment the cloud passed and he blinked a couple of times. "Oh, yeah—that Willie Marino guy was there."

"Who's that?" Mother asked.

"He's from—let me see if I can remember the name of it. . . . I think it's called Admiral Dis— No, that's not it. . . ."

"Admiral General Distributors?" I said, a sinking feeling in the pit of my stomach.

"That's them!" he replied brightly. "They're the ones that market the tapes."

For some reason I had the feeling that marketing in this case had something to do with breaking arms and fitting cement overshoes—but then again, my entire knowledge base for organized crime comes from movies of the thirties and forties.

"Willie's around a lot," Jeff continued. He leaned in toward the three of us and added conspiratorially, "Between you, me, and the lamppost, I think he liked to watch." He sat back in his chair, which let out a metallic groan. "You must've seen him."

This had me totally perplexed. "Where would we have seen him?"

"At the party at Derrick's house."

"He was there? Which one was he?"

"You *had* to have seen him," Jeff replied with an impatient roll of his eyes. "He sticks out like a sore thumb. He's a really good-lookin' guy. You seen him . . . you remember? He was talking to Derrick when you asked me who Derrick was. The guy in the gray suit."

I could feel my eyes widening. The man in the gray suit. The one who'd looked out of place because his mode of dress and his manner were both so businesslike. I hadn't known anyone from Admiral General Distributors was at the party. It meant that a member of the Mob had been present when we were asking questions about Patrick, and when we'd made our appointment with Brett. It meant something else, which made me feel afraid for the first time since we'd been attacked in the alley behind the bar: it meant that Marino, who apparently worked for the Mob, most likely had known who we were from the moment we set foot in that party. After all, we'd had to give our names at the door and they were written down by the leather queen on guard at the door. Many of the subsequent events clicked into place.

"Was Marino there when Patrick and Brett performed together?"

Jeff shrugged again. The action was beginning to annoy me, because it made me think I might've been wrong about him. Maybe he'd had values at one point and had to shake them off his shoulders every time they tried to re-land.

"He was there when I did it. I don't know how long he stayed."

There wasn't anything else we needed to learn from him, so we rose and started for the door. Mother and Peter stepped out onto the walkway, and I hesitated in the doorway. I took Jeff's hand, an action that seemed to startle him.

"Look, I really don't think you should go on working for Mano Man."

"Why not?" said Jeff, his eyes growing wide.

I shook my head wearily. "Jeff, it's just not safe. There's something going on there. I don't know what it is, but I know it's dangerous."

He started to protest, but I cut him off. "*You* know it's dangerous. For God's sake, two guys are dead."

"That don't have nothing to do with me." His eyes had

become vacant again, and I knew it was a lost cause. I didn't know if he was too afraid to face the facts, or too afraid to face a possible change. But I knew the warning was no use. We said good-bye and left.

"Well, that's that, then, isn't it?" said Mother as I drove our little company back to the hotel.

"Is it?" I replied gloomily.

"It seems obvious, darling. This Marino person was there when Patrick mentioned the CIA."

"We don't know that."

"I think we can assume it. He heard what Patrick said. He's with the distribution company being investigated by the government. So, Marino heard what was said, realized he and his company were in danger, and then killed Patrick and Brett Lover. Or had them killed."

"And Marino was at the party," said Peter, "which explains the attempt on our lives on the way home."

"But . . . why kill Brett Lover?" I said, feeling more and more dissatisfied. "Just because he heard Patrick, too?"

Mother pursed her lips. "I think it more likely that they followed us and shot Brett when they saw he was going to talk to us."

"Yeah," said Peter, warming to the idea, "it's obvious they've been following us, because we were attacked outside that bar—the Peacock."

"An attack that was interrupted very conveniently by Ren Forrest," I countered. We fell silent for a moment; then a new idea came to me. "Maybe . . . maybe that means that Ren Forrest is also part of the Mob." I turned to Peter. "Didn't you get the feeling he was trying to warn us off?"

Peter nodded. "Not too indirectly, either."

"But that doesn't make sense," said Mother. "These people don't exactly shy away from killing. Why on earth warn you off instead of just having done with you? They certainly could've shot you at the pier, when they killed Lover."

I thought about that for a minute. "Well, if they really do think we're with the CIA, they might not have wanted to kill us because it would bring the CIA down on them."

"I see," said Peter, nodding slowly. "So they just killed anyone who they thought was talking to us. Except . . . except that doesn't explain the attempt on our lives on the way home from the party."

"I know, I know," I said, my mind spinning.

We fell silent again for a few minutes, each of us lost in his or her own jumble of thoughts, trying to work it out. Mother finally broke the silence.

"You know, all this still only leaves us with Willie Marino. We know he was there the day Patrick mentioned the CIA, and he's the only one we know of directly connected with Admiral General Distributors."

"Uh-huh," I said dully, my mind occupied.

Mother huffed in exasperation. "Do you have any doubts about Marino being the murderer?"

"Oh, no. Not at all."

"Then what's the trouble?"

I sighed. "It isn't enough to *know* who did it if he's never caught."

"I agree," said Mother warily, apparently already unhappy with where this was headed, "but don't you think that's something to leave to the professionals?"

"You mean like Nelson?" Peter was unable to hide the distaste in his tone. "I got the impression he was much more interested in continuing his investigation than in catching the man who murdered two faggots."

"Not Nelson necessarily," said Mother. "We could take our suspicions to Detective Furness."

"According to Ren Forrest, the police already know about the Mob connection to this, and they know when to look the other way."

Mother replied in her haughtiest upper-crust British accent, "If Mr. Forrest is also in the Mob, I *hardly* think his word is unimpeachable."

"Perhaps," I replied, "but Furness referred to these porn stars as 'disposables' and Nelson called them 'unfortunate.' I'd much rather depend on someone who thinks all human life is worth something. Like us."

"Alex," said Mother warily, "you can't seriously be thinking of taking on the Mob! Are you out of your bloody mind? I'll not have you committing suicide." She looked as though she'd kill me first.

"I'm not talking about taking them on. But maybe we can find proof that Marino is the killer."

"And how do you propose to do that? March into Mr. Marino's office and say, ' 'Scuse me, luv, but did you happen to kill a couple of young men?' I'll be having you picked up and thrown in Bedlam."

"Oh, don't go all Dickensian on me," I replied irritably.

"Your mother's right, Alex," Peter chimed in. "This is too big for us."

"I wasn't talking about confronting Marino. For God's sake, I'm not an idiot! I'm just talking about trying to get evidence of his guilt. If we can do that, then Nelson or no Nelson, *Furness* isn't going to let a killer get away."

"How do you expect to find evidence? Unless Marino

is a total halfwit, he's not keeping a log of who he's killed each day," said Peter.

I sighed wearily. They were chipping away at my resolve, even though on a purely primal level, I was determined not to let two murders go unpunished. Finally, I said, "Well . . . maybe you're right. Maybe there's no evidence anywhere that he's a murderer. But we might be able to find evidence of his Mob connection, and that might be just as good. If we can't get him put away for murder, maybe we can get him put away for something else."

I think this was really the first time in my life I'd ever seen my mother go red in the face. She took a deep breath to calm herself and tried to reason with me without further losing her temper. "Darling, I know you're upset, but you have to think about what you're suggesting. Surely you realize that if this Marino person is responsible for two deaths, any hint from you that you're investigating them will be suicide."

"Maybe . . ." I admitted reluctantly.

"And if you won't think of your own skin, think of who else you'll be affecting."

"You and Peter will—" I started, but she cut me off.

"Not *us,* darling. If Marino's the killer, he already at least *suspects* there's something wrong at that video company, if he doesn't know it for sure. If you do anything to confirm it for him, however innocently or well-intentioned, he might decide to cut his losses and get rid of everybody concerned."

That really did bring me up short, in the most frustrating way. She was right. I felt like I had nowhere to turn, while at the same time I wanted to run in all directions at once.

"For God's sake, I can't just sit and do nothing!"

Mother nodded sympathetically. "We can go back to the hotel, have a nice dinner, and sleep on it. See if our heads are clearer in the morning. Maybe then we can think of a less fatal way to proceed."

Sleeping on it would have been a great idea if I'd been able to deaden my brain, but by the end of our dinner in the hotel restaurant, I knew that wouldn't be possible. All the way through the meal, the various people we'd questioned kept popping into my mind, like a psychotic episode from a forties movie. I was sure that if I tried to let it go for the evening and went to sleep, I'd have one of those Salvador Dalí nightmares, like Gregory Peck had in *Spellbound*.

We were done eating before six, and by that time I'd made a decision. Mother and Peter might be right about the folly of butting heads with the Mob, but I was right, too: I had to do something. And the safest thing I could think of, for the time being, was to case Marino's lair.

As we exited the restaurant into the lobby, I told Mother to go up to her room without us. I was, of course, assuming my husband would come with me.

"Why?" she said, stopping abruptly.

"Oh, I just want to ask the concierge about something and maybe pick up a pack of cigarettes," I replied. I could feel my cheeks redden. God, I wished I could be more like my mother when it comes to stretching the truth.

"Alex . . ." she said with a touch of warning in her voice.

"I just need a little smoke to help me relax." I yawned disingenuously and added, "I'm *soooo* tired."

One corner of Mother's mouth went up, the other went down, and there was a hint of a sparkle in her eye.

"Very well," she said, and after a slight hesitation she headed for the elevator.

Peter turned to me and said, "What are you up to now?"

"I'm not going to get any sleep tonight if I don't do something. I just want to find Marino's company and maybe have a look at it. What can it hurt?"

"Our arms, our legs, and various other parts of our anatomy," he replied, reluctantly following me to the information desk.

One of the perks of staying in a really classy hotel is that the concierge has to locate things for you. We asked the young woman at the desk to look up Admiral General Distributors for us, and she pulled out various phone books and quickly made her way through them. She was so striking that I was now convinced that L.A. really is manned entirely by male and female starlets.

"Aha, here it is," she said, thumping the book with her manicured index finger. A look of concern straight out of chapter 2 of *An Actor Prepares* creased her lovely face.

"Are you sure that's the place you want?" she said.

"Admiral General Distributors. Uh-huh, I think so," I replied.

She squinted at me as if she suspected that I wasn't really a guest at their hotel.

"Okay," she said, "here's the address."

She scribbled it on the notepad and handed it to me. The company was located on Workman Street, which I'd never heard of.

"Where is that?" Peter asked.

She pulled out a map and flipped it open, peering at it with all the grim concentration of Vanna White. Then she

210

tapped a spot with her fingernail and said, "Here it is, by the river. It's way into the city."

She said this with a rueful smile that was meant to convey her embarrassment at having to direct a guest to such a place.

I wish I'd taken the hint.

SIXTEEN

Peter was all for waiting until the next morning to do this, seeing as how our day had already been pretty full (to say the least), but I was too pumped to wait.

"I just want to check it out," I explained lamely.

We got on the Santa Monica Freeway and headed east. The endless L.A. rush hour was taking its toll. Traffic moved at a snail's pace, when it moved at all.

We exited at Alameda, as per the concierge's instructions, and headed north. This area was much more congested than Santa Monica, and it was definitely dustier and hotter, being farther from the ocean. I saw at once why our intention to come to this neighborhood caused such a stir with the concierge: from what we could see from Alameda, the side streets were peppered with huge, lumbering buildings. And even with all the traffic you got the impression of general desolation. Given the number of cars flowing out of the side streets, anyone with a brain was scattering from the area like half-drowned fleas from a dog that had just jumped in the river.

About a half a mile or so up Alameda, we found Workman Street, and I hung a right.

"God, can't the Mob afford a better neighborhood?" said Peter, his forehead wrinkling with concern. "This can't be the right place."

Just before the street was cut off by the river we found the address we were looking for. I circled around and parked about half a block down. The place was an enormous, rambling box of a building made of what looked to me like post–World War II corrugated tin. There were barred windows along the side, very high off the ground that would prevent any improbable passersby from looking in. The whole building looked like it would fold up like a beer can at the first tremor, though given its conspicuous age it must have withstood far more than that.

It had taken us so long to get to the building that it was now well after seven, and the area was deserted.

"That can't be it," said Peter.

"But it is. Look at the sign."

Above one of the doors was a small wooden plaque that bore the words "Admiral General Distributors."

"That's a warehouse," I said stupidly.

"Your grasp of the obvious is astounding."

We sat staring at the building for a minute; then, as if impatient to get me away from the area before I did anything stupid, Peter said, "Well, we've seen it."

I ignored him. "I wonder . . ."

"What?" said Peter.

"Well, you remember what Jeff Durkin said at the party?"

214

Peter heaved a sigh. "He said a lot. And he was high."

"No, I mean when I asked him about where they filmed. He said they filmed at Holmes's house, and that he thought Holmes had a warehouse someplace, too."

Peter looked at the building, then back at me. "So?"

"It's just that it didn't occur to me at the time, but he mentioned the warehouse when I asked about where they *filmed*. I think he meant that they also filmed in a warehouse."

Peter thought about this. "Well, that could be, sure. But that doesn't mean it's this one. And what difference would it make, anyway?"

"I don't know. Maybe none at all. But I suppose if you really wanted to investigate the Mob, the best thing to do would be to get them to let you use their facilities. I mean, then you could search the place when they weren't there."

Peter shrugged. "Well, either way, I can't believe Marino works in there."

I was staring at the building, a new idea growing in my mind. There were a couple of cars around, but nothing outstanding and nothing that looked as if it were specifically there for that particular warehouse. As idiotic as that sounds, it's the way I was thinking at that moment.

"Alex? Did you hear me?"

"Huh? Oh, yeah. But I don't want to waste the trip. I have an idea."

"I don't think I'm going to like it."

"I'm sure you're not going to like it. I think we should . . . go in and have a look around."

"Are you fucking nuts!" said Peter with an uncharacteristic lapse in language. "You want to break into a warehouse owned by the Mob?"

"Well, for crying out loud, we've already broken into the house of a man we thought was connected with the Mob."

"But he wasn't!"

"But we didn't know that at the time!"

We looked at each other for a minute. Peter clearly did not like the idea of doing this, but his expression told me that he was pretty sure I'd do it on my own. In this, he was mistaken: I don't think I would have gone in there without him.

"All right," he said as he reached for the handle of the passenger door, "but I want to go on record as saying I'm doing this under protest."

"Oh, you'll love breaking and entering," I said with a wave of my hand. "Mother and I do it all the time."

I knew that Peter's initial reluctance to accompany me into the warehouse was a sign of neither cowardice nor indifference. He was as anxious to find Patrick's killer as I was, and he's probably a lot braver than I am. But he also has a good deal more common sense than I do.

We made a wide circle of the warehouse to get the lay of the land. The fortunate thing about the high windows was that while they didn't allow us to see in, they didn't allow anyone to see out, either. We went around the side on the cross street, where there were three large docks with those towering doors that slide upward. We continued around to the back of the building and found two doors that I assumed to be emergency exits of some sort at either end of the building.

We tried the first door and found it locked, so we went to the second and tried the knob. Fortunately for us, it was open.

"That must mean there's someone here," said Peter.

"Not necessarily," I whispered in reply, "They may just be careless. After all, who in his right mind would break into a Mob warehouse?"

"*We're* doing it."

I looked back at him. "I rest my case."

With that I turned the knob as quietly as possible, and the two of us passed through the door.

It was not exactly cool inside, but it wasn't anywhere near as hot as it was outside. We could hear the loud, steady whir of several large fans attempting to augment the feeble air-conditioning.

"There *must* be somebody here," Peter said softly. "They wouldn't have left all this stuff on if the place was deserted."

"There aren't a lot of lights on. They probably just have a guard on duty or something. We just need to be quiet."

We went along the back wall. On our left was row after row of shelving units, towering from the floor to the ceiling with an occasional cross space to provide access from aisle to aisle. We started down the last aisle, stopping now and then to check out the contents of the shelves. There were stacks and stacks of porno videos of every type imaginable, gay and straight, along with pornographic books and magazines and several other forms of paraphernalia the likes of which I'm happy to say I'd never seen before. At one point Peter reached into a crate and pulled out a thick rubber penis that had to be at least ten inches long. He grimaced.

"A veritable pornucopia," he whispered as he replaced it.

The variety of tapes was astounding, and I know it will

sound ridiculous given the tenor of our lives over the past few days, what with the porno party and the porno actors and Peter's auspicious audition, but seeing all this stuff in one place really made me feel soiled. I guess my threshold for soiling had risen way past where it should be. I made a mental note to lower it as soon as this case was over.

We made our way down the aisle in the relative darkness until we reached a cross-aisle that divided the first half of the warehouse from the second—sort of a porno-equator. We rounded the end of it and continued along the shelves by the wall. We'd gone about half the length of the warehouse when I stopped.

"Did you hear that?" I whispered.

"What?"

"I thought I heard something."

We stood there for a moment, straining to hear any sign of movement above the loud whoosh of the fans. I looked at Peter and shrugged, figuring it must've been my imagination (or my nerves) that had produced the sound, when suddenly we heard a faint but definite noise from the front of the warehouse. It was no more than the scraping of metal, as if a chair had been pushed back or pulled out.

I looked back at Peter, raising my eyebrows in question, and he nodded his assent. We quietly continued down the aisle, trying so hard to hear that my ears were beginning to pooch out. The only noise seemed to be the sound of somebody walking around, and voices muted by the rushing air.

The end of the aisle was partially blocked by a black wall about eight feet tall. When we reached it I realized it was a flat: fairly flimsy panels of plywood that stretched in a semicircle around an open area, which appeared at the end of the shelving units like a glen in the middle of an industrial metal forest. We hung back and peeked through the open shelves.

"What is this?" said Peter.

"A set," I replied. "Look."

It was, indeed, the type of setting one sees occasionally in porn videos—a flat black room with no furnishings that adds to the anonymity. In this type of room, which appears to exist in someone's warped imagination, sexual fantasies are acted out on a platform or the floor. A card table and a couple of folding chairs were set up just inside. The area was lit only by an overhead worklight, which gave the setting the feeling of a death chamber at Dachau.

"I really need a bath," said Peter.

Whoever had been there wasn't there now, but we could still hear somebody in the distance, presumably down a hall beyond.

"What do we do now?" Peter asked.

"Wait until whoever's back there goes away, then look around."

We were prepared to do just that when someone unexpectedly walked onto the set from the opposite end, closely followed by another man. The first was Derrick Holmes; the second, I immediately recognized as the man in the gray suit we'd seen talking to Holmes at the pretty-party: Willie Marino. This time he was dressed in a dark blue suit (I somehow thought pinstripes might be more appropriate) and was carrying a briefcase, which he dropped with a slap onto the table. Marino didn't have any of Holmes's dubious heterosexuality: instead he emitted a threatening straightness that seemed to beckon you closer so it could strike.

Though we'd originally thought that the openness of the shelves was an asset, we suddenly decided that the danger of our being spotted was too great for us to remain there. I motioned to Peter, and we ducked behind the first flat. Fortunately, at the end of the first panel was a crack wide enough for us to peek through without being readily seen.

"You got the money?" said Holmes.

"Yes," said Marino slowly. His thumbs were resting on the twin latches to the briefcase, as if poised to open it. He paused and looked up at the director. "You know, Derrick . . ." He drew Holmes's name out distastefully, as if to him the director's first name was a synonym for "faggot." "I've heard that you've been having a little trouble with your . . . staff."

"God," I whispered to Peter, "he sounds like Nelson."

"What do you mean?" said Holmes without emotion.

"You know what I mean," Marino replied gravely.

Holmes smiled sardonically. "I can handle anything. You know that."

This reply seemed to please Marino. "We just don't like having any attention drawn, you know."

Holmes's smile grew a bit more ominous. "You've picked a pretty high-profile business, then, haven't you?"

I couldn't tell from my vantage point exactly how Marino had taken this.

"I just wouldn't like to think that there are any special . . . problems here. My business associates wouldn't like that."

I got the weird feeling there was some sort of test going on here, though its exact nature eluded me given the cryptic way it was being carried out.

Holmes didn't budge. He said, "Everything's taken care of."

If it was a test, Holmes had passed. Marino's thumbs twitched and the latches on the briefcase popped open. I half expected the thing to explode. He turned it toward Holmes. I saw the contents just briefly. It was stuffed with money.

"I think we're witnessing the big payoff," I whispered to Peter.

"Then the feds should be glad we're here to witness it," he replied softly, "We're about as impartial as they come. We'll probably have to appear at the trial."

"Oh great," I replied, "I can see it now: 'Faggots Finger Mob.' We won't be alive when it comes to trial."

Holmes reached into the briefcase, his usual lack of expression marred by a slight, satisfied smile. He pulled out one bundle of bills and said, "It's a living."

Marino was on his way out even before the words left Holmes's mouth, as if he'd already had more contact with the porn director than he wanted. I wondered if he'd head straight to the nearest Catholic church for one of those mobster confessions you see in bad movies. Then again, in the movies they only go to confession when they murder somebody.

Holmes was thumbing through the stacks of bills when I heard a soft "pong" behind me, then a thud. I swung around anxiously and was about to warn Peter to be quiet when I unfortunately got a practical demonstration of what had made the sound: a pipe came down on my head.

SEVENTEEN

At first I was aware of only a low mumbling that seemed to come from inside my head. I had the sensation of being underwater without being wet. When I tried to raise my arms they wouldn't move. I was tied to something. Other voices began to intermingle with the mumbling, which I suddenly realized was coming from me. It took an effort to stop. At first I was afraid that I'd been doing loudly, but as the other voices became clearer, I was relieved to find that they hadn't noticed. As my awareness grew, a wave of pain washed over me from the knot on my head where I'd been hit.

"I told you they'd come here! Didn't I tell you they'd come here?" said a slightly familiar and very excited voice through the painful fog that seemed to have drifted between my ears.

My head lolled sideways; at the same time, I realized it would probably be better if I didn't move. Not knowing the situation yet, I wanted to keep as still as possible in hopes I'd be able to pick up something from whoever was talking. I did manage to sneak a stealthy peek at as much as I could of my surroundings without moving my head. I was sure that I was on the black, blank set. "I've seen this movie before" came into my head, and for one panicked moment I thought I'd said it aloud, but the voices went on without a beat.

"Didn't I tell you they'd come here?"

"Yeah, you told me," came the rumbling growl that I readily recognized as belonging to Derrick Holmes.

This made me wonder at once why we were tied up, given that Holmes worked for the FBI. Then again, presumably he didn't know who we were and that we were on the same side, or a different faction of the same side. It also came to me in a fragmented memory that one of the last things I'd seen before being conked on the head was Willie Marino walking out of the room. It was entirely possible that he'd come back. Worse yet, it was possible that we hadn't been as clever as we'd thought in hiding behind the set, and Marino had spotted us. In that case, he was probably the one who attacked us.

Either way, I was afraid we'd inadvertently put Holmes in the position of having to play out whatever role was necessary to maintain his cover as a pornographer and Mob pawn. I couldn't imagine that he'd be happy with our blunder, and I didn't want to imagine what was going to happen next.

"I done good for you, didn't I?" said the excited voice.

"Yes, you did."

"Well . . ." The voice hesitated. "Well, do ya think I could have some stuff, then?"

There was a marked hesitation on the part of Holmes, then he said with a curious tone in his voice, "Sure. Sure. In a little while."

Peter chose that moment to groan. I wasn't happy that he was hurt, but I was sure happy to know he was alive.

"Ah, they're coming back to us," Holmes rumbled.

"Whaaa?" said Peter.

"It's all right," I said quietly in his direction. I slewed my eyes sideways and saw that Peter was next to me, tied to an uncomfortable wooden chair. I raised my head and found myself face to face over the expanse of the floor with Derrick Holmes. He was dressed in a Hawaiian shirt and tan shorts that revealed cascades of body hair, which made him look like a tourist from the Planet of the Apes. Beside him on a tall canvas director's chair sat Willie Marino. Oh God, I thought, we'd made things worse for Holmes (and for ourselves) than I'd even supposed. Marino's presence explained why Holmes had had to tie us up. Marino sat with one serge-suited leg crossed over the other, his large hands resting on the arms of the chair, which looked like it would buckle beneath them. Another figure hovered in the background, in the darkness behind the video cameras.

Marino looked past us as he spoke to Holmes, giving the impression that none of the occupants of the room were of any significance to him.

"Like I said, we're not happy with the way things are going with your company here. It may be time for us to sever . . . relations."

Holmes looked neither scared nor impressed. "I told you, I'll take care of it. I can handle this. I'll find out who these guys are and what they're doing here. Then I'll take care of them. That should prove to your boys that I'm reliable."

Marino said nothing, but moved his head ever so slightly in Holmes's direction. I realized right away that Holmes had made a fatal error: Marino had seen us at the pretty-party. He knew something was wrong.

"Leave them to me and I'll take care of them," said Holmes, oblivious to the recognition from Marino.

Marino sat silently for a moment, then slid one leg from the other and slipped off the chair. "Sure," he said without expression, "you do that."

Marino left the "stage" in the same direction as he'd exited when we were watching from behind the set. Holmes continued to stare at us for a moment and seemed to be waiting for something, which he heard. A door opened and closed from the direction in which Marino had gone. Holmes didn't smile.

"Is he gone?" said the figure that was still hidden by the darkness behind the cameras.

"Um-hm."

"Are they awake?"

"Come and see. Come on." Holmes beckoned as if talking to a child.

The figure stepped into the light. To my astonishment, it was Jeff Durkin.

"I told you they would come here, didn't I? They asked about Willie. They asked about Admiral General Distributors, and I knew they'd end up here." He sounded just like an overanxious puppy.

"Um-hm," said Holmes noncommittally.

"I did good, didn't I?"

Holmes didn't look at Durkin, but I got the impression that he felt Durkin was more like a gnat than a dog.

"You did right," he said after a pause that anyone with unaltered senses would have realized was a cue to shut up. Jeff Durkin didn't take it that way.

"So can't I have some stuff now?" he said, a little more pathetically.

Holmes finally looked at him. "I said later."

Even Durkin got the message that time. He dropped cross-legged on the floor next to the director's chair, for all the world as if awaiting the bidding of his master. If one of my arms had been untied, I would have hit myself in the forehead. That perpetual vacant expression of Durkin's was chemically induced, and even though I'd thought he was high at the party, I hadn't realized he was hooked.

Holmes stepped over to the director's chair and lifted himself into it as if it were a throne, never removing his eyes from us. He crossed his legs in a curiously feminine way that I was sure would give him rug burns, with all that hair. He folded his hands in his lap and sighed.

"So, what am I going to do with you?"

"We could make a movie," I said, unable to disguise the sneer in my voice. I couldn't help it: even if this jerk was working for something the feds considered the greater good, I couldn't get past the fact that he was using my people to do it.

"I don't make snuff films," he rumbled without expression.

God knows this startled me. I didn't know how far he was going to play this, or exactly what part Durkin had in this little drama. I figured that probably Holmes couldn't drop his cover as long as Durkin was around, but I wasn't sure. I thought it best to find out.

"So," I said with a nod toward Durkin, "does he work for the same people you do?"

"Him?" said Holmes with a muffled snort. He reached down and stroked Jeff's hair once or twice. "No, he just does little jobs for me. Like keeping tabs on people I need to know about. Like you."

I glanced down at Durkin, but the scorn on my face went unnoticed. Durkin's slightly sweaty face was turned up expectantly at Holmes, who didn't bother to return the attention.

"Don't get me wrong. He doesn't follow people. My little Jeff isn't quite smart enough for that, I don't think. No, he just reports to me what he hears. When you started asking questions about Patrick Gleason, little Jeff here came straight to me. And he carries out some errands on occasion, for little considerations."

"Like parts in your movies? So he gets fucked over both ways?"

Something resembling a smile fought its way through the fuzz on Holmes's face. "No, he gets paid for his performances. He gets little presents for keeping an eye on people, don't you, Jeff?" Holmes reached into his pocket and pulled out a small white packet. "Like this."

At the sight of the packet Durkin perked up immediately, and he seemed to sweat more profusely. It was a pathetic sight: Holmes holding the packet above the hopeless young man, held at abeyance like a dog with a biscuit on its nose, waiting for the signal to snatch it up.

"He'll do a lot for this," Holmes added needlessly.

I tried to hide my disgust. "So in addition to making porno movies, you're supplying drugs?"

"Oh, I don't supply the drugs; my associates do."

"To you," I said angrily, "but you supply them to *him*."

"I don't charge him," said Holmes with a shrug, and with this he dropped the packet, which Durkin caught and tore open greedily. He pulled a thin tube out of his pocket, stuck it into the packet, and inhaled. I managed to spare a thought for how foolishly I'd tried to give him words of wisdom. Like Patrick, this guy was beyond hope. My batting average was unimproved. I didn't much watch Jeff after that.

"Jesus," said Peter under his breath. I was glad to hear he'd come around enough to realize what was going on around him.

"Look," I said to Holmes, still trying to keep from saying directly what I was talking about for fear of arousing Durkin's interest. After all, Durkin knew Willie Marino, and I no longer entertained any sort of hope that Durkin was redeemable. I was sure he'd go straight to Marino if he had information he could barter. He couldn't help himself. "Look . . . I know who you are."

"Everybody knows who Derrick is," said Durkin unexpectedly. He appeared to be calming down considerably.

"I mean," I said more pointedly, "I *know* who you are."

There was another rumble from within Holmes's mammoth beard. I knew he was smiling somewhere in there.

"And I *know* who you are," he said mockingly. "You're with the CIA."

"Oh." I glanced down at Durkin, who was singularly

unimpressed. He was too busy taking care of his other nostril.

"If you knew we were with the CIA," said Peter indignantly, "then what the hell was that audition of mine all about? Why the hell didn't you just talk to me?"

Holmes replied evenly, "I wanted to see how far you would go. We're all trained never to blow our cover. I wanted to see if you'd take my dick up your ass to keep yours. That would have been sweet. I would have fucked the shit out of you if your . . . mother . . . hadn't shown up."

So that's why he'd sounded so amused: he'd known who Peter was all the time. Waves of disgust washed over me. A lot of us feel like we're being screwed by the government. Holmes acted like he thought it was his right to make it literal.

"How long have you known who we were?" I said, trying to dispel the visual images Holmes had caused.

He let out a snort. "You know how long. What I don't know is how you got on to me."

These words hung there in the dusty, fan-swept air of the warehouse like a slowly blinking sign in a liquor store window: "how you got on to me" . . . "how you got on to me" . . .

The only reply I could think of was "What?"

Holmes didn't move. "I should've known the minute your friend showed up and said he'd been talking to the CIA that it was all over, but I thought maybe if I got rid of him, everything would be all right. At least for a while."

There was another silence. I managed to say "What?" again from somewhere in the stupor I felt descending into my pounding brain.

"Alex . . ." said Peter warningly. I could tell by his tone

230

that he was now wide awake, and probably about five minutes ahead of me in figuring out what we were hearing.

"I should've known. . . . I should've known," Holmes repeated wistfully, "that once you guys got on to me, everything was over. I should've gotten out then."

"Why didn't you?" said Peter suddenly.

There was a little snort from the beard. "Because Malibu has a way of getting into your skin."

"You got that right," said Durkin dreamily.

As always I found it really irritating that Peter had figured out something and left me behind. I sounded petulant when I said, "Would somebody please explain to me what you're talking about?"

Peter turned to me, and I saw his face for the first time. The muscles were tight: he, too, was experiencing a great deal of pain from where he'd been hit on the head. He sighed in an attempt to relieve it.

"He thought Patrick was talking to the CIA. He 'severed' their connection."

I looked at Holmes, whose lack of expression almost made my circulatory system grind to a halt. I realized at that moment that this guy had murdered my old friend and Brett Lover, and that he looked about as remorseful as John Wayne Gacy in a clown suit. And he had us tied up.

"You killed Patrick?" I said impotently. "Why?"

Holmes gave an appreciative "Humph." "They trained you really well," he said. "I could almost believe you don't know. But I know better."

I looked to Peter, who was staring at Holmes fixedly. Peter said, "My guess would be that Holmes killed Patrick because he thought Patrick was our connection to him."

"The CIA investigation," I said slowly. "He thought we were part of the CIA investigation?"

"Um-hm."

"Then . . ." It was beginning to come to me, and I felt like the class-A clod I was. The CIA investigation—the investigation we were endangering and that Larry Nelson was working on—they were investigating Derrick Holmes.

"Bingo," said Peter, a rueful smile in his voice. He'd noticed the look on my face and knew I'd figured it out.

"It was slick," said Holmes, "the way he dropped the CIA into the conversation when we were filming. Really slick. But I don't know what you hoped to accomplish."

I could feel bile running down into my stomach. Nausea churned around down there and threatened to slip back up to my throat. It had all been a mistake. It had all been a really stupid, stupid mistake that had snowballed and cost Patrick his life.

"We weren't trying to accomplish anything. We weren't here to investigate you. We were trying to get Patrick out of porno movies. That was all. Patrick was an old friend of mine."

"Sure," said Holmes.

"Why would the CIA be investigating you?" said Peter.

"I know you know about the money. There's no use denying it. Why else would you have been here tonight?"

The money. I glanced at Peter, and from the look he shot back from the corner of his eye I could see he had no idea what the director was talking about, either. The first we had heard or seen of any money was that briefcase that had changed hands earlier. Except— Oh, God, another thought came to me, and I shoved it down. I didn't want any sign of recognition to escape to my face.

232

"So you killed Patrick . . . and you killed Brett Lover?"

There was a slight nod.

"But why?"

"Because he was going to talk to you. We tried to get rid of you, or at least warn you . . ."

"In the car when we left your party," I said.

There was another nod.

" 'We'?" said Peter.

"One of my associates, and my little friend here," Holmes replied with a gesture toward Durkin.

"Oh, man, that was a blast!" said Durkin airily, rocking back and forth on his butt like a happy child. He closed his eyes and seemed to lose himself in a world of his own. Or maybe he was just reliving the fun of almost killing us.

"So what are you going to do now?"

"Sever the remaining connections," Holmes replied with a frightening lack of emotion. "The two of you. And your mother." There was an electrified pause before he added, "By the way, where *is* your mother?"

I could feel myself going pale. "I have no idea. You don't think I'd bring her to a place like this, do you?"

"Not if she was really your mother. Then again, it doesn't much matter who she is. I'll take care of her soon enough."

My mind frantically raced for something that might buy us some time, and it suddenly lit on *Goldfinger*.

"What good would killing us do? You know if we disappear all hell will come down on you. You'll never get away."

"That's where you're wrong," said Holmes, and I thought I could detect something of a smile once again fighting its way out through the brush around his mouth.

233

"There will be a pause, however brief, in the proceedings."

"What do you mean?"

"It will take them a little time to realize they've lost you, and to send somebody else out. That pause will give me the window of opportunity I need to get out of the country. Even if it's only a little window. Killing you will buy me the time I need."

So he didn't know about Nelson, who would know we were gone pretty damn quick. And he didn't know Nelson was really the one investigating him. But that didn't matter. Holmes believed we were his immediate problem. Even if I told him about Nelson now, I was sure he wouldn't believe me. And if he did believe me, I'd just be signing Nelson's death warrant, which like him or not I wasn't prepared to do.

I decided that, if we were going to be killed, I wasn't going to make it easy on this prick. I calmed myself and attempted to devoid my face of expression.

"You're wrong about buying yourself time," I said confidently.

There was a slight hesitation. "What do you mean?"

I tried my best to sound like an authentic agent instead of like an overpaid government delivery fag. "The CIA may take a while to realize we're gone. But you'll never get out of the country."

"Ha. Who's going to stop me?"

I paused for effect, then said, "Willie Marino."

Holmes paused, but not for effect. His expression didn't change, but the beat before he responded told me that I'd hit the mark.

"What do you mean?"

"You made a mistake," I said, attempting a superior smile, "earlier, just before he left. You made a mistake, and Marino noticed it. I saw him do it. Didn't you, Peter?"

"I sure did," Peter replied with an air of confidence that surprised me, since I was pretty sure he didn't have a clue what I was talking about.

"What?" said Holmes, his gravelly voice tinged with harshness.

"You told him you'd find out who we are. You acted like you didn't know us. But he knew that wasn't true. He's seen us before."

There was a silence, during which the director appeared to be running through his memory. After a few moments, the negligible bit of his face that wasn't covered with hair grew white, then flushed red. "The party," he said.

"That's right."

"Willie was at the party," Durkin chimed in, still rocking back and forth, "he was at the party in that beautiful silk suit. God, I wish he was gay! I'd throw my legs over my head for him!"

"Shut up!" Holmes snapped. Durkin complied but continued to rock and smile.

Holmes slid a gun from behind his back, apparently having had it tucked inside his belt. There were small beads of sweat forming over his brows.

"It can all be explained," he said more to himself than to us. "I can explain it away. I can say I was keeping an eye on you myself . . ."

"But he knows you lied," I said evenly.

As if adding an exclamation point to what I'd just said a door closed at the far end of the warehouse: not a slam, mind you, but just loudly enough to let anyone within earshot know that whoever had come in didn't particularly care whether or not he was heard.

Holmes's head snapped in the direction of the sound and he raised his gun like a vice cop.

"You stay here and watch them," he said to Durkin with quiet anxiety. Jeff didn't give any sign of having heard him. Holmes carefully moved to the first aisle, at the opposite side from the one we'd used. Staying close to the wall, he started down the aisle, quickly disappearing from our view.

Peter and I watched the corner of the shelves until we had some hope that he was far enough away that we could whisper without being heard. I glanced at Peter, then turned to Durkin and said, "Jeff, untie us!"

Eyes closed, Jeff began to hum.

"For Christ's sake, Jeff! Untie us!"

Durkin's lips parted, and a gust of breath escaped him. "It makes me makes me makes me . . ." he sang, off key but keeping somewhat to a tune I remembered as "When it says Libby Libby Libby on the label label label."

"Jeff, snap out of it!" said Peter as sharply as he could without raising his voice.

"I love it love it love it . . ." he continued to sing as he slipped his right hand down the front of his pants. "Oh man, it do feel good. . . ."

"God, what are we going to do?" I said to Peter.

"What would Indiana Jones do in a situation like this?"

I almost laughed. "I can't imagine him being held prisoner by a drugged-out idiot playing with himself." I turned back to Jeff to try again. "You don't know what a mess we're in. I mean, what a mess *you're* in."

"It feels good good good . . ."

"Jeff, please try to understand what I'm saying."

His eyes suddenly popped open and he said dreamily, "I understand you, man."

"No you don't," I said frantically. "Your friend Derrick Holmes works for the FBI, or he did. He's done something to screw them over—"

"Oh yeah, he's good good good . . ." sang Jeff. He slowly got to his feet and, still keeping the tune going, pulled down the zipper on his shorts.

"And he's screwed over the Mob at the same time! And you're in the middle of it! Don't you get it? If you don't untie us so the three of us can get out of here and get help, either Holmes or his Mob boss is going to kill us!"

Durkin's eyes closed again as he slid his shorts down and began stroking himself, "You worry worry worry . . . don't worry worry worry. . . ."

"Jeff, please!" I implored.

"Oh, I don't believe this!" said Peter with exasperation, "We're going to be executed in front of a peep show! I can just see *those* headlines!"

"This is hardly the time to worry about what people will think!"

"Jeff . . ."

Durkin swayed left and right in front of us while he stroked himself more rapidly. "Oooo . . . God, that's good. . . ." he purred in his best porno-movie voice.

At that moment, I noticed movement in the darkness around the far end of the flat, the end from which Willie Marino had left the warehouse.

"Slow it down . . . slow it down . . . slow it down. . . ." Jeff gave up all pretense of a tune as he got more into himself.

The figure stepped from the darkness at the edge of the

flat and came into the light, behind and a little to the left of Durkin and carrying with it a short piece of metal pipe. It was my mother.

I hoped that I didn't look as astonished as I was for fear that Durkin would open his eyes and realize that something was wrong. But I didn't need to worry. He continued his routine and repeated, "Slow . . . slow . . . slow it down." At this, Mother lowered the boom.

"Glad to oblige," she said as Durkin dropped to the floor. "You *do* know the most charming people," she said to me with a cluck of her tongue.

"My God, you've knocked him out!" I exclaimed stupidly.

Mother curled her lip at me. "Did you want me to wait till he finished his performance?"

"For God's sake, what are you doing here?" I said.

"Honestly, look at the two of you," said Mother as she laid down the bit of pipe and crossed behind us. As she began to untie me, she added, "It isn't safe to let you walk the streets alone, is it?"

"What are you doing here?" I said, more sternly.

"I followed you, of course," she replied matter-of-factly. "It wasn't hard, and even if I'd lost you, I still knew where you were going. I watched you talk to the concierge, then asked her where you'd gone."

"Not that I should be unhappy to see you under the circumstances, but it's far too dangerous for you here!"

Mother nodded her head, and I could see over my shoulder that her face was dripping with sarcasm, "Oh, I can see it's too dangerous for *me!*"

"Will you just untie us?" I snapped.

"There's a little bit of hurry-up involved here," said

Peter, "since at the moment we have a rogue FBI agent here searching the place for a guy from the Mob. We heard him come in."

"Oh, you mean the door?" Mother said in her primmest Mary Poppins voice. "That wasn't the Mob coming in; that was me going out!"

"What?" Peter and I said in unison.

"I told you I followed you here. I got up to the end of that shelf over there just about the time they were tying you up. When you started telling him about Willie Marino being on to him—by the way, that was an inspired bit on your part—"

"Thank you," I said dazedly.

". . . anyway, I thought it best to stir things up a little, at least to distract him long enough to get you the hell out of here. So I went back to the back door and made sure I closed it loud enough to be heard. I felt sure he'd investigate. Then I just nipped around the outside to the front door, slipped in, and here I am."

"Are you out of your bloody mind?" I said.

"Well, it worked, didn't it?"

"But you could've gotten yourself killed!"

"And you most definitely would have been killed if I hadn't done something!"

"Do you think," said Peter crisply, "that you could possibly postpone this family squabble until you've untied me?"

"Oh," said Mother, coloring slightly. "So sorry." And in another moment she had him freed.

"We've got to get out of here. Holmes is wandering the aisles with a gun. It's not gonna take him long to decide to come back here." I turned to Mother and added, "Do you have a gun?"

"I didn't pack a rod this trip, darling. I didn't think we'd need firearms to get Patrick out of the movies. I suggest we head out through the door I came in."

A low groan emanated from the inert form of Jeff Durkin as we tiptoed past him and around the far corner of the flats. There was a fairly dark space past which lay a short hallway. One side was the outer wall, the other an office with semi-opaque glass windows. At the end of the hallway to one side was the front door to the warehouse: the door we'd bypassed when we arrived, in favor of the more obscure entry in the back.

Mother came to an abrupt halt at the door, with Peter and myself slamming into her like an extremely mismatched version of the Three Stooges. She shot a withering glance over her shoulder at the two of us, then, as quietly as she could, opened the door a crack. She peered through the opening at the dusty twilight and uttered an "Oh Lord!" Peter and I squeezed in beside her to look. Derrick Holmes was standing in the middle of the open area between the warehouses, looking from side to side. It appeared as if he'd just about satisfied himself that nobody had come into the warehouse and was trying to figure out where whoever had closed the back door had gone so quickly.

Just before we shut the door, Holmes wheeled around and headed back toward the warehouse. He stopped in his tracks when he saw that the door was ajar and, after a brief pause, hurled himself in our direction like a wild thing, letting off one shot in the process that popped through the wood just above Peter's head.

"Jesus!" he exclaimed. Mother slammed the door and turned the dead bolt. I grabbed a straight-backed wooden chair from the end of the hallway and shoved it under the doorknob. I had no idea what that was supposed to do, but that's how they always secure a door in the movies. There was one split second of silence, followed by the crash of Holmes's body hurtling against the barred door. An unmistakable splintering noise assured us that locks and chairs notwithstanding, Holmes would be with us in a matter of moments.

"This is not a good situation," she said, sweeping to the side of the door in case Holmes should let off another shot.

"Let's get the hell out of here!" I said, and the three of us ran for the back door.

Even in my panic I managed to notice that Jeff Durkin had rolled up into a fetal position, a pool of some unmentionable-looking mass lying beside his head. He had apparently roused just long enough to vomit before returning to his unconscious state.

We fled down the far aisle, toward the sideways shelves that bisected the room. Just as we were about to round the corner, there was a subdued rumble as the front door shattered and our pursuer tumbled in. I grabbed Mother by the arm to stop her and held a finger to my lips. Peter stopped just short of running into us again. There was no further sound, but I swear to God I could *feel* Holmes's presence in the building. Staying perfectly still you could almost sense the stale air of the warehouse shifting around him as he approached.

From the look on Mother's face, I could tell I wasn't the only one who'd developed this sense. She whispered sternly: "Okay, quickly and quietly," as she led us around the shelves and down the aisle to the back door.

When we reached it, I grabbed the doorknob and

turned it, but the door held fast. Holmes had locked it. Peter said, "Look," and pointed to the lock. My stomach dribbled down into my shoes when I saw why Holmes had been so intent on breaking through the door in front. This particular lock was the type that requires the key to unlock it from either side. And since it opened inward, it would be a hell of a lot more difficult for us to break *out* than it had been for Holmes to break *in*. We were trapped, and he knew it.

"Oh, shit!" said Mother, her choice of expletive serving as a sure sign the situation was truly dire. Mother doesn't swear easily.

At that moment a shot rang out from the opposite end of the warehouse. The three of us looked at each other, and I imagine that the expression on my face showed the same amount of shock as on theirs.

"Split up," said Mother.

"Wait!" I cried as quietly as I could.

"It's the only way!" she countered. She slipped down one aisle, and with a nod at me, Peter slipped down another. In horror movies the heroes always make the mistake of splitting up, and that's what gets them all killed. But Mother's logic was unmistakable: staying together made us sitting ducks, but Holmes couldn't be in three places at once, so our chances of finding some way to immobilize or evade him were higher if we were apart.

Mother had gone left and Peter went right. I stood plastered against the end of the middle row of shelves, trying to decide which way I should go. I didn't relish the idea of starting down an aisle only to find myself face to face with a man with a gun with the nearest crossway several yards off. The fans continued their noisy hum, providing the only sound.

I craned my neck around the corner of the shelves, and felt only slightly relieved to find the aisle empty: now I knew one place Holmes wasn't, but still had no idea where he *was,* or from where he might emerge. I crossed the aisle, sticking to the back of the shelves, and glanced down the aisle just to the left of center. It was also empty, so I decided to take my chance.

I walked as quickly as I could without making any noise. I was about two yards from the first cross space when I heard another shot. My heart lodged in my throat. I plastered myself against the shelves as someone ran along the bisecting row. It was a moment before I realized that the brief flash of material I'd seen streak across the space was my mother, and that meant that she at least had made it half the length of the building. But the sound of the shot and the speed of her retreat indicated that Holmes was in hot pursuit.

I knew I had to distract him, and a quick glance at the shelf I was pressing against gave me an idea. I shoved a box back through the shelf. It pushed against a box on the other side, which hesitated only a moment before slipping off and dropping to the floor of the center aisle.

I tried to flatten myself against the shelves again in a desperate attempt to disappear into them while staring down toward the opening I'd seen Mother race across. Holmes came just into view, gun in hand, as the box fell. The noise stopped him in his tracks. Instantly he wheeled back and started down the aisle behind mine. I breathed a sigh of relief—but it caught in my throat when I realized that Holmes would surely know almost at once that the crate had been pushed from my side. I charged for the back end of the row, desperate to get out of this aisle before Holmes reached the cross space. I almost made it.

Just as I reached the corner, a shot rang out and pinged against the corner of the shelves. I didn't even bother to glance back, remembering the lesson learned through repeated viewings of *Chariots of Fire:* if you look back at your pursuer, you lose time. Unfortunately, this left me with a dilemma: I didn't know whether Holmes would continue down the aisle or opt for a crossway. Neither way looked good for me. In trying to distract him from Mother, I'd cornered myself.

I stayed pressed against the end of the shelves so that I couldn't be seen, but it wouldn't take him long to figure out what had happened to me. I agonized about which way to go with the heightened desperation of a hunted animal. Suddenly there was a loud crash in the aisle down which Peter had run. I was surprised at first, then it hit me: Peter and Mother must have gotten onto how I'd distracted Holmes, and were now doing the same.

I took the opportunity to glance down the aisles on either side of the shelving unit: Holmes had continued down the aisle in which I'd fled. Unfortunately for me, he appeared to have caught on to the purpose behind the crash, and wasn't going to fall for it again; but it had startled him enough that he was looking the other way when I glanced around the corner, and I managed to race to another aisle before he turned his head.

I knew now, or at least believed, that Peter and Mother had managed to get past the raving FBI agent, which was at least some consolation. However, I was still trapped in the back half of the warehouse, near the door that required a key. Even if Mother and Peter made it out the front door, they still wouldn't be able to open this one to free me. With Holmes knowing my approximate whereabouts, it would be difficult for me to get by him without being seen through the shelves. It would only be a matter of time before Holmes had me, unless I came up with something or Peter and Mother found some way to come to my rescue.

That's when I had the brainstorm that demonstrated for once and all that I'd lost my reason. Throwing aside the one hard and fast rule Agent Lawrence Nelson had taught me for avoiding pursuit—never go up—I decided my best bet for eluding Holmes was to try to scale the shelves. If I could reach the top without creating a lot of noise (hoping that any noise would be masked by the steadily droning fans), Holmes just *might* believe that I'd somehow managed to get past him.

I gripped the highest shelf I could reach, lifted a foot up to get a hold of one below, and began to climb, carefully pushing the pornographic debris away from the edges as I went to ensure that I didn't make the mistake of knocking anything to the floor. There was less than an inch of ridge bordering each shelf, which made my sweating hands slide precariously with each grasp, seriously cutting into my hold and my confidence: with each new shelf as I climbed the metal network that spanned to within a few feet of the ceiling, my hands gripped and slid on the metal. My body was uncomfortably arched in the center, the shelves between my hands and feet jutting into my stomach as I tried to balance myself.

I had achieved the halfway point when, with my next step, the shelf creaked and bent beneath my feet. I hoped the noise wasn't really as loud as it sounded to me. I held my position for a moment, and the fans seemed to hesitate in their revolutions, as if holding their breath in anticipation of my being found out. At that point, I didn't think there was anything (other than my sagging strength) to keep me from continuing the climb.

I passed shelves of cartons and crates of tapes and rubber and plastic implements that had "Marital Aids" tattooed on the side. I was getting dizzy from the exertion and panic, when my right hand finally reached the top shelf. I reached as far across it as I could while my legs continued the rest of the way up. I was just about to swing my legs up when a shot rang out and a hole popped through the top shelf about three inches from my head.

"Fuck!" I said under my breath, though the low tones were no longer necessary, since it was obvious that Holmes knew where I was. I lay stock-still against the heavily painted metal of the shelf, silently breathing in the heavy dust that had settled there and cursing myself for not having listened to Nelson. I raised my head enough to see the lay of the land. There was a veritable sea of shelf tops, close enough to make it possible to jump from one to the other, but far enough apart to make doing so dangerous. I thought I could manage the jump, even without being able to stand fully erect, but I knew I couldn't do it quietly. And then there was the possibility that if I miscalculated, I would go straight to the cement floor.

Whatever I did, I had to do it fast, because although Holmes had paused in his shooting, I could be pretty sure he hadn't stopped. I decided the best thing for me to do was to slide myself forward as far from my current position as possible along the shelf before jumping. I thought that would at least confuse Holmes as to my location. Though the shelf top was littered with crates, I was pretty sure I could get around them without being seen. I slid forward, trying not to make a sound, realizing that this was the first dusting this thing had ever received. I had gone a few feet when another shot rang out, and another hole popped through the shelf in between my ankles.

Sweat was now pouring from my forehead, turning the dust to mud, as I pulled myself along faster. In my mind's eye I could see Holmes way down on the ground, staring up at the shelf, trying to detect any movement. When I'd gotten to the next section of the shelf, I drew up my knees and rotated onto my feet, into a crouching position. I stayed that way for a moment, eyes closed, trying to stir up my courage to leap to the next set of shelves. Finally I decided it was now or never. I opened my eyes, and my heart ground to a halt: a pair of hands were appearing over the top of the opposite shelves. In a blind panic, I glanced behind me at the shelf top against the wall. Unfortunately, it was only half as wide of the one I was on, and I was sure if I tried to jump and grab hold of it, that would be the last thing I ever did. I was just short of letting out a terrified scream when Peter's head popped over the top of the shelf. The force of the relieved air escaping from me was almost enough to knock me off my perch.

Peter hoisted himself onto his shelf, smiling and waving at me as if we were meeting at the beach. We launched into an argument held in pantomime. If anyone had happened upon us, they would have thought they were seeing a movie whose soundtrack had snapped.

"What the fuck are you doing up here?" I mouthed.

"Confusion," his lips moved back at me, as he bared his arms.

"What?"

"Confusion. Mother's gone for help—we have to keep him busy." He pointed down toward the floor. "Watch."

Without another word (I should say without moving his lips again), Peter leaped across from his shelf to the next, so that he was one row over from me. I realized at once what he was doing. After giving Holmes what I thought was enough time to react, I peeked over the side of my shelf into the aisle behind me. It had worked. Holmes had heard the noise and realized there was something wrong with it.

He edged his way around the corner of the cross space. I could almost read his thoughts as he hesitated: he was wondering why the noise had come from such an odd distance. With a slight shake of his head, he continued through the cross spaces, and when he'd just about reached the bottom of the row on which Peter was now crouched, I pushed a crate off the shelf and it went crashing down to the floor, bouncing back and forth against the shelving as it went.

Holmes wheeled around and let off a shot without thinking. Peter looked across the expanse of shelves at me and raised his eyebrows. He had managed to get farther down his row, and when the noise of the falling crate had stopped and Holmes was beginning to retrace his steps, Peter jumped to the next row of shelves. Holmes stopped in his tracks and I drew back just before his head turned up in my direction.

"I know you're up there!" he bellowed, his voice sounding odd and disjointed at the increased volume.

No shit, I thought.

"You know you can't get away from me!"

Peter waved at me and pointed to the shelf on which he crouched. He was indicating a large cardboard box. He smiled and pushed it off the shelf. Below another shot rang out, and I thought I heard it ping against metal just before one of the overhead lights shattered, sending shards of glass flying in a flurry of sparks that burst like a skyrocket and fluttered down.

I felt a sudden pain and grabbed my left arm. Red beads sprouted in a line and spread until they formed a stripe of blood beneath my hand. A shard of glass had grazed me as it flew by. I glanced over at Peter, whose concern was evident on his face. I mouthed, "I'm okay," at him, and he sighed in relief.

After a moment of silence, Peter and I seemed to realize simultaneously that there was a curious scurrying sound coming from below, accompanied by the unmistakable clamor of boxes being pulled from the shelves. Peter gestured toward the cross space at the end of my row of shelves. As carefully as I could, I slid over, inched to the edge, and looked down. I knew in one alarming moment exactly what Holmes was doing. He had apparently gotten the idea from the brief burst of sparks from the lightbulb: he was spreading magazines and cardboard around the bottom of the shelves. He was building a bonfire.

I could feel how stunned my face looked. I turned back to Peter and mouthed across the expanse, "Joan of Arc!"

Peter's eyes widened and his lips moved. I didn't even have to guess what he'd said.

I could already smell the smoke. Holmes had hit on the perfect plan for getting us: if we came down, we'd be shot;

if we stayed here, we'd be cooked. I'd been right when I told Mother that whoever had murdered the porn stars was spinning out of control. I wasn't sure that Holmes realized that whatever happened to us, he was probably cooked, too: I had to believe this place was stuffed with cartons, printed material, videotapes, and crates, all highly flammable material that would burn down in a matter of minutes. And if that didn't kill Holmes, the Mob surely would.

That's when it hit me: the crates. Though they were outnumbered by the cardboard cartons, there were still a few wooden crates up here atop the shelves: the crates marked "Marital Aids."

The closest was on the next shelf. I leaped over, got behind the crate, and pushed. Holmes had heard the movement and let off another shot, but I managed to get the crate over the edge without being hit. It crashed to the ground, missing Holmes by a mile.

I looked at Peter, whose eyebrows were raised in question, and with the worst attempt at sign language you could imagine, tried to get my idea across to him. Somehow he got it. Rather than trying to elude Holmes, we needed to draw him to us.

Peter leaped to another shelf with a clamor. His foot slipped as he caught the shelf and for just a moment I thought he might slide off to his death. We had more than two ways to die in this fiasco. But he righted himself in time and pulled his way onto the shelf. He was now two aisles away from me. From where I was I could see Holmes slink through the cross space, his California-clad frame backlit by the flames. It made him look like Satan on a vacation. I jumped to the next shelf, so I was directly across the aisle from Peter and I pulled back out of sight just as Holmes whirled around in my direction, his face upturned. At that moment Peter pushed a crate off his shelf, and with an unfortunate amount of noise it fell to the ground. Holmes got out of its way in plenty of time. He laughed out loud, and we could still hear him chuckling as he started to light another fire beneath Peter's shelves.

I looked at Peter and shook my head. There was no way we'd be able to get a crate to fall fast enough to hit the crazed FBI agent before he got out of the way. Peter shrugged and grimaced, indicating that we didn't exactly have a lot of options here.

There was one crate a few feet behind me, and with the reluctance of someone who has realized he's chasing smoke, I got behind it and pushed it as quietly as I could toward the cross space. On the ground below, Holmes was tossing more debris on the fire, with so much glee I almost expected him to cackle. I was just about to push the crate over the edge when I thought I saw a slight movement at the far end of my row, at floor level where the building was bisected. I narrowed my eyes and peered in the direction of the movement, and finally made out the figure of my mother. She glanced at the arson-bent form of Holmes; then her eyes found me, and she appeared to take in the whole idea at once. She turned a palm up to me, signaling that I should wait a moment.

There was the sound of flames, sparks popping upward as they were spread by the huge fans, and the sound of the fans themselves. I held my breath. Then Mother looked up at me and nodded. I pushed the crate over the edge.

Just as I pushed, Mother yelled, "Hey!" at the very top of her lungs.

Holmes jumped up, wheeled around, and let off a shot in her direction as she disappeared around a corner. That moment was enough to distract him from the noise overhead. It wasn't until the last minute that he seemed to sense the movement. His face snapped upward right at the moment that the crate made contact, and he crumpled beneath the crate, which burst open on impact, sending its contents, a bevy of oversized dildoes, cascading in every direction like a shower of obscene worms.

"I guess he's fucked," said Peter.

EIGHTEEN

You realize, of course, that you destroyed an FBI sting that took months to put into operation," said Agent Lawrence Nelson, though he didn't sound exactly upset about the whole thing.

"I can't tell you how sorry I am to put the government out of the porn business," I replied.

To say we'd put an end to it was putting it mildly. We'd managed to get out of the warehouse before it was completely gutted by flames, just as Detective Furness arrived. Mother had called him and Nelson from the warehouse office while Peter and I were doing our high-shelf act. She'd come back into the warehouse proper when she heard the shots and the noise of crashing crates, and that was when I'd spotted her.

We'd also managed to drag Jeff Durkin from the warehouse, but only so his body could be given a decent burial. There was a bullet hole through his head, apparently from the first shot we'd heard fired. Holmes had been leaving nothing behind in his mop-up mission. Everything else, any link between the government and the Mob, had gone up in smoke. We hadn't even been able to retrieve Holmes's body before it was engulfed in flames.

It was now much later that night, and we were gathered in our room at the Hotel Windemere by the Sea for a much-needed drink and much-needed explanations. Agent Nelson hadn't gone far in the way of chastising us. In fact, he seemed pensive, and relieved that the whole mess was over. Especially since all the evidence had burned.

"I hadn't expected you to discover that Scott Keller—Holmes—was working for the FBI. Although given past experience, I might have expected it."

"You should've come clean then," said Mother scoldingly, "If you had, the whole thing would have been a lot less dangerous."

"Not with your boy, here," said Nelson with a rueful glance in my direction. "I was afraid if he knew the truth, he'd wouldn't just let us handle it. I thought he'd rush in and blow the whole thing."

"Which he did anyway," said Mother, "*because* you wouldn't tell us what was going on."

Nelson took a smooth drink of his Scotch, the first alcohol I'd ever seen him consume, and stiffened. "I told you more than I should have, and you know that. You should have trusted me, accepted that the Agency was doing what was necessary."

"Only what was necessary from *your* standpoint," said Peter disdainfully. "We couldn't be sure that your idea of justice was the same as ours."

Nelson thought about this for a moment without altering his expression. I chose to take his silence as tacit agreement. He then turned to me and said, by way of changing the subject, "So when did you learn that Holmes had gone rogue?"

I could feel myself blushing. "When we were tied up."

Nelson didn't comment on this. "But you did manage to figure out about the money."

"Only after he insisted that we knew about it."

"What money?" said Mother, and I realized she must have missed that part of the conversation.

I replied, "Holmes insisted that we knew something about 'the money,' and that was why he thought the CIA was investigating him. It took me only a minute to remember that our friend Nelson here had said he was investigating the transfer of funds overseas."

"So it wasn't just a mistake," said Mother, putting it together, "when Holmes thought the CIA was investigating him—you really were."

Nelson nodded and sighed. "Only he didn't know that until the three of you happened in, and . . . someone mentioned the CIA. That was all Holmes needed to hear to think we were on to him."

I turned away from him. I was truly ashamed of the slip I'd made and the repercussions it had caused. To my astonishment, Nelson's tone was somewhat conciliatory as he said, "But I've made mistakes, too, in my time. We just try to make sure they don't happen again."

I looked at him. He wasn't smiling, and he wasn't threatening. He simply looked as if he was certain his point had been made. I nodded at him.

Nelson then turned to Mother and said, "Chances are, all things being equal, he would've eventually figured out that we were investigating him. But we hoped by then we'd have him."

"I still don't understand that part," said Peter. "How *did* you get on to him to begin with?"

Nelson shrugged noncommittally. "Checks and balances. And a little of the right hand not knowing what the left hand is doing. Admiral General Distributors was selling overseas. We keep a close eye on them and everyone connected with them. In our surveillance, we found that someone connected with them—Derrick Holmes—was transferring large sums of money overseas. Presumably the money he made from the videos. While investigating him, we discovered that he was working for the FBI, and the money he was transferring was supposed to be going into a slush fund to pay for the operation."

Peter said, "Holmes said that 'Malibu has a way of getting under your skin.'"

"Exactly," said Nelson. "The life the FBI had set up for him to do the sting was too alluring. Like that Sherlock Holmes story, 'The Man with the Twisted Lip' . . ."

I tried to hide my surprise at hearing that Nelson read Arthur Conan Doyle.

". . . he found he could make much better money joining the business than he could by exposing it."

"Oh Lor," said Mother. She looked blank for a moment, then shrugged and sipped her tea. After a short silence, she perked up and said, "Who was it that searched my apartment?"

"I imagine it was Holmes," Nelson answered uncertainly.

"But why?"

"I think I can answer that one," I said. "Holmes found

out you were connected with us at Santa Monica Pier. And he might not have known where we were staying, but he knew where *you* were."

She blinked at me, then smiled. "Jeff Durkin. Of course!"

"Exactly."

Mother thought about this for a moment, then turned to Nelson. "Larry, why did you ask me to watch Patrick Gleason?"

Nelson glanced at me, and I got the impression he was about to offer a practical demonstration of the fact that even at this stage of his career, he could make mistakes.

"That was an error on my part. Of course, after we'd started to investigate Holmes and Mano Man Productions, we knew everyone connected with them. We knew Gleason was one of those people, but didn't think he was . . . important. So I didn't think it would hurt, as long as you were interested in seeing him anyway, if you kept an eye on the goings-on at his apartment."

Mother looked perplexed. "But you didn't recognize Patrick's name when I called you. You didn't say anything about it until you called me back."

"Um, yes, that's true. But that was because though it was a CIA investigation, it wasn't *my* case."

"Whose was it?" I asked.

Nelson took another drink from his glass, set it on the table, and said, "The man you know as Ren Forrest."

"*What?*" Peter and I exclaimed in unison.

"We . . . detained the cameraman who was originally working for Holmes. Then Ren Forrest showed up on cue and wormed his way into the job."

"Oh, my God," I said, still in disbelief. "Then it *wasn't*

a coincidence that he showed up when we were being attacked behind that gay bar! He was following us."

Nelson looked just a little embarrassed. "Well, no, it wasn't a coincidence, and you weren't really attacked."

"That's funny," said Peter, curling his lip. "I distinctly remember having a knife shoved in my face."

"And being rescued in the nick of time," Nelson countered. "Ren thought it best, since I couldn't convince you to leave, to try to scare you into thinking it was too dangerous for you to continue."

"Oh, great!" I said sharply, "We were almost killed when our tire was shot out from under us, and almost killed behind the bar, and both times it wasn't the Mob threatening us, it was our own government! That's just great."

Nelson sighed. "I still contend that the FBI's original sting operation was worthwhile, though it did have some . . . unfortunate side effects."

I rolled my eyes and when they'd dropped back to earth I noticed how bitter Peter looked. I felt the same sense of bitterness, but I was a little—just a little—inclined to think that Nelson might have a point. If only they could trust their own people.

"What about Willie Marino?" asked Peter. "And the Mob connection. Will it just be business as usual for them now?"

"Since Mano Man Productions has been dissolved with such . . . finality, I have no idea what the FBI plans to do about Marino and company."

Mother took another sip of tea. "I wonder what the FBI will have to say about our putting an end to their little escapade?"

258

Nelson looked at the three of us in turn, downed the remainder of his Scotch, and stood. "Nothing."

"Nothing!"

He flashed a knowing smile at us and said, "Nothing."

"You mean we won't be in any trouble at all?"

"More than that, I'm sure there was never an FBI investigation into the connection between the porn industry and organized crime."

"Look, Nelson," I said, rising from my chair, "I don't know what you're trying on now, but—"

"I'm sure," he continued pointedly, "that if anyone was to look into it they'd find there was absolutely no evidence of any investigation whatsoever. Thank you for the drink."

He started toward the door, but I stopped him.

"Larry, what about the CIA? Would we find any evidence of a CIA investigation into Mano Man Productions?"

He smiled. "Enjoy the rest of your vacation."

With that he walked out the door.